ORCAS TEETH
A tale of a space pirates.

By Graham A. Rhodes

First published 2018
Internet Kindle Edition 2018

GRAHAM . RHODES 5@ BTINTERNET.COM

Templar Publishing Scarborough N. Yorkshire
Copyright G. A. Rhodes 2018

Conditions of Sale.

This book is sold subject to the condition that it shall not, by way of trade or otherwise, be lent, re-sold, hired out, or otherwise circulated without the publishers prior consent, in any form of binding or cover other than that in which it is published.

Dedication

This is the first book in the Space Pirate series. As usual it would have been impossible without the help and encouragement of the following people –

Yvonne, The Badgers of Bohemia, Tubbs & Missy, Steve Dickinson & the Scarborough Sci-Fi Convention, Dave, and Ysanne in the hope that one day it will turn up in her bookshop.

ORCAS TEETH
Graham A Rhodes

Chapter One

In a parallel universe on the far side of a distant galaxy, in a solar system very similar to our own only even more dysfunctional, a three-masted space cruiser flew along a long forgotten space lane linking a distant moon to its equally forgotten planet. It solar powered sails hung limp, shredded by the effects of a very unfriendly sonic laser protecting a mineral shipment from the mines of Vega, fired by someone willing to fight to keep it.

It wasn't the smartest ship in this or any other universe. Its paint was faded and peeling off, showing bits of rusty metal. If it was in a second-hand ship dealer's showroom it would be classified as the bottom of the range, and sold in the yard around the back, although a more observant inspection might reveal that it held some surprises underneath its bonnet. For one thing it held a very efficient photon drive and one or three other customised "improvements" not normally found on such models.

Its engines strained and the ship seemed to roll slightly, caught on the prevailing solar winds. The flight deck and observation deck were deserted, mainly because the Captain and crew were below decks. It would be unfair to say they were sleeping off the effects of a particularly nasty hangover, as they were not asleep. They were seated around the map table in the Captain's cabin. The radar scanner beeped loudly and four heads rose from their prone position on the table top and groaned in unison. An empty bottle rolled across the star chart and made its way to the edge of the table. It would have fallen to the floor if the navigation officer hadn't spotted it and lifted one of his arms. His metallic hand opened out and the vice like fingers grabbed the falling object. It shattered in the tight grip, scattering bits of glass over the floor. The Captain raised his head so it was almost at right angles to the rest of his body. He tried to focus his one good eye.

"Too hard... your grip's too hard!"

The navigation officer looked down on his metal hand and opened and closed it a few times. Bits of glass fell from it.

"Can't seem to control the squeezy thing properly" he muttered.

The Captain looked at his navigation officer whose name was Star. He had no idea of his real name, or his race. He looked even greener than usual, and he wasn't sure if the red lines around his eyes were natural. He watched fascinated at a red flashing light that seemed to pulse on Stars round bald head. Then he realised he was looking at a reflection from a blinking light on the control board behind him.

The Captain tried and failed to remember something about red flashing lights. All he could remember was that it was something important. It was a red light. Something in the back of his mind told him that blinking red lights were even more important. He tried harder to remember but his attention got waylaid by a strange gurgling sound coming from his engineering officer. She was sitting opposite him with her head held very firmly in both her hands. Very firmly! She was only well aware that in her current state, any sudden movement would result in her dropping it and her head rolling along the cabin floor. She didn't want that to happen again. She let out another strained gurgle.

"I do wish you wouldn't do that in public Edith!" The Captain said.

The head in Edith's hands looked up and blinked its eyes. "I need to clear my head. There's a damaged circuit in there. My wiring feels like a Malovian Dredge Worm had made a nest in there and is trying to bore its way out."

Before The Captain could say anything there was a slight click and Edith lifted her own head up and carefully placed it back on her shoulders. She gave it a twist so it was pointing in the right direction and placed her hands behind her neck where she twisted a fastening and it all clicked back into place. She turned it one way and another, looking around the room.

"I'm not convinced that sampling our prize haul was a good idea!" She said.

The fourth member of the crew lifted his head from the table. "You've got to taste it. It's part of the job. If we don't know how good it is we won't know how much to sell it for."

The three of them looked at Cat Face, the ships weapons and artillery officer. His yellow eyes were tiny vertical slits and his nose and whiskers twitched. He looked slightly greyer than usual but, as his name implied, as he was to all intent and purpose, a large, grey furred human cat, it was difficult to say.

Edith looked at him with a shocked expression on her face. "You mean someone will pay good credits to drink that stuff?"

Cat Face grinned, showing his two small white fangs. "It's the finest Pulovian Brandy!" he protested.

"No it's not! It's what you get when you mix an equal amount of very cheap brandy with equal measures of mark three propulsion fuel and....."

The Captain paused and lifted his glass. He sniffed at it. ".....cough medicine!"

"Finest Pulovian paint stripper more like!" Star said. He focused on the light at the opposite side of the room. "By the way why is that light blinking?" They all turned to look at it.

"I was wondering about that!" The Captain murmured.

"It's either an engine malfunction in the lower deck or the bulb is on the blink." Edith observed.

"Shouldn't you find out?" The Captain asked her. He'd just remembered that red lights were a warning. Flashing red lights were an urgent warning.

Edith rose to her feet and walked across the cabin. The Captain watched her walk and stifled a little sigh. She had a very attractive body, but she was an android, with limited moving parts. As far as species went she wasn't a woman, she simply looked like one, which was even more frustrating. He watched as she stopped in front of the blinking light, bent down to examine it and brought her fist down on it very hard. The light stopped blinking.

"Is that a good or a bad thing?" The Captain asked.

Edith turned and shrugged her shoulders.

Star gave a grunt and put his non mechanical hand to his head. "There's something following us!" he said.

The Captain turned to him. "How far away?"

He didn't need to ask how Star knew. He knew Star just knew. Star was a "sensitive". There were a few of them scattered across the universe. Usually their natural talents and services ensured highly paid positions in many military organisations and corporations. For a start they saved a fortune in sophisticated technological navigational equipment, but unlike the equipment "sensitives" were more accurate. He often wondered why such a talent was wasting his time on a second rate, pirate ship operating in the outer fringes of the known universe.

Over the years The Captain discovered why it was called the outer fringes. It was because no one bothered to go there. It was the perfect safe haven for a space pirate with little ambition and, as The Captain was eager to point out, in his line of business ambition could prove dangerous to one's health. The ripped sails were a testament to that.

He looked back at Star. "It's not that trigger happy transporter come to have another go at us is it?"

The Navigation officer shook his round head causing a series of double chins to wobble. "We left them behind three days again. They won't follow, we're too far off their schedule. No profit for them."

The Captain rose to his feet. "Flight deck everyone. I've a bad feeling!"

"It's his Pulovian paint stripper!" Edith muttered.

The flight deck wasn't anything to write home about, if indeed anyone did actually write anywhere anymore. The main controls were worn and slightly grubby. The place needed a thorough cleaning. However that duty fell to the Engineering Officer, and as Edith pointed out that now, in the thirty third century of the Fall of the Imperial Nest, women should not be regarded as drudges. They were expected to be of equal rank and not cleaners. She hadn't undergone and passed all the required examinations just to end up as the ships cleaner. The Captain pointed out that she wasn't a woman, she was an android. Edith retaliated by saying "female android". The Captain then pointed out she actually hadn't sat any exams, that she had been programmed with the knowledge. She pointed out that she still knew her way around the ships engines better than anyone else and, if he was so clever he could engineer the ship himself! The point was taken. He then tried to install a rota, but that fell apart when Stars mechanical hand proved unsuitable for the delicate job of dusting. After his first attempt they had to call into a service station on the far side of somewhere they didn't want to be to get it fixed. The Captain winced. He was still making the repayments on that repair. Fifty five old credits every moon. He sighed. One day the rightful owner of the Universal Credit Card issued by the Bank of Snakeheads on the planet Onerous would discover someone else was using it. There again maybe not. You never know your luck. Perhaps the real owner had died in some galactic accident, or war. There were enough of them going on. Off planet there were a thousand ways to die, none of them very nice, but all of them equally fatal, which was why he liked to operate out here on the long forgotten space lanes. Only it seemed they weren't long forgotten. Something else was out here, and it was following them, which brought his mind neatly back to the present.

On the flight deck all eyes looked towards the largest screen in front of them. In the centre there was a blip. The indicators showed that not only was it following them on the same course, it was gaining on them.

"How long before it's in range?" The Captain asked.

"His or ours?" Asked Cat Face.

"Knowledge of both could prove useful!" The Captain replied, trying and failing to sound sarcastic. Anyway sarcasm was lost on a cat.

Cat Face slid into his weapons pod, slung underneath the flight deck. He took up his firing position in front of a small bank of monitors and a number of switches and levers that were the firing controls. He pressed buttons and numbers and calculations danced across the screens in front of him.

"He's out of our range!" he shouted up at the flight deck.

"And?" The Captain responded.

"I've no idea what weapons he's got so I can't work out if we are within his range or not. If it will make you happy I can say that if he's armed with one of those latest photon beamed sonic whatsits he can blow us out of space in around......" He paused and did a quick calculation, ".......an hour and ten minutes!"

The Captain swore.

"Incoming!" Edith suddenly shouted.

The Captain swore again, only louder. "I thought we weren't in range?"

"It's not coming from there". Star replied.

He flicked a couple of switches and the screen changed. Now they could see a second blip. It was in front of them. They could see the streak of the missile as it headed towards them.

"Evasive action!" The Captain said and grabbed hold of the ships wheel. He planted both his feet firmly on the deck and pushed the wheel forward, sending the ship into a downward dive. He fired up the secondary engines and everyone hung onto whatever wasn't moving towards the far end of the flight deck.

"What about the screens?" Cat Face shouted up from the weapons pod.

"Full screens!"

The Captain spun the wheel violently to one side then dragged it screaming upright. The ship changed direction. Now it was going up and all the loose stuff that had passed them when they hung on now passed them again, travelling in the opposite direction. Everyone gritted their teeth and held on. A flash illuminated the flight deck.

"Missed!" The Captain said.

"Shot down!" Corrected Star. The Captain looked across at him.

"Whoever is following us didn't like the idea of a missile heading in their direction. They blew it out of space. Which is good. What isn't so good is that we now know we are within their range."

"Time to go!" The Captain said.

He punched a couple of buttons and then punched them again when nothing happened. When he heard the drive engage he pulled back a small lever. The air around them throbbed. In the space where they had been a slight glow appeared. Ship, no ship. Now they were somewhere else. It was a neat trick and had got them out of trouble on more than one occasion. He had found the drive in the wreckage of an old burnt out fighter ship they had come across drifting in the vastness of space. Its hull was torn and the cockpit shattered. They had found the remains of the occupants spread across the ship.

There wasn't enough of them left to identify what race they were, or had been, but judging by the shape of their seating arrangements and the fact that they found more than a few claws, they assumed they were a lizard like race. The writing on the documents and consuls was just a series of shapes. They had salvaged all they could, including a strange drive that, after a deal of sweating and swearing, they had dismantled and attached to their own solar wind powered drive.

The first test had been spectacular. It took them a full two days to find out where the new hybrid drive had taken them. Since then they had experimented and refined its controls so now at least, they reappeared in the same galaxy.

Pressing the engage button was a bit like participating in a game of Russian roulette. You knew the ship would take off, but you never knew where you would end up. On the up side The Captain was pretty sure that no other ship had one, apart from the race that invented it of course, and as he had never heard of a lizard race, let alone come across them, he figured he was alright. He would have liked to have said it was the secret of his success as a space pirate, but he couldn't. He wasn't that successful.

He looked across the flight deck to Star. He was slightly less green now. More his usual damp moss colouring. Star knew the question before it was asked. He shook his head.

"I didn't get time to enter our last known coordinates."

He scanned his screens and then closed his eyes. After a few moments he opened then again. His Captain was still looking at him. He checked his screens once again.

"I've no idea where we are, but we are not alone."

"Don't tell me they've followed us!" The Captain said as he turned to look at his own screen.

Star leant forward and pointed a green blobby finger at a different screen. "See that planet?"

The Captain looked where the finger pointed.

"Now look behind it!"

The Captain looked. There was a series of small white dots that pulsated as they moved across the screen.

"That's a war fleet if ever I saw one!" Star said.

"Whose?"

They turned to see Edith standing behind them.

Star shrugged. "No idea!"

The Captain looked down at the weapons pod. "Are all our shields up?" He asked.

"Invisibility screen deployed!" Cat Face replied.

The Captain turned back to the master screen. "Let's watch and see where they are heading."

"And then set off in the opposite direction?" Edith suggested.

"Let's see." The Captain replied.

They shadowed the fleet for almost a week during which time Star managed to work out where they were. Then, when they knew, they wished they didn't. They were in a region where the Dominion of Dave bordered onto the region ruled by the Kingdom of the Stella Knights. No one on board had ever heard of the area or the boundary before. Neither had anyone heard of the two groups of peoples until they ran a computer check on them.

The on-board ships computer had recently undergone a major upgrade during their last planet fall and, due to a misunderstanding with the download instructions, had ended up with a pink type face and a female voice that the instruction manual described as "Ancient Brummie English." They had no idea what "Ancient Brummie English" sounded like but they did know they didn't like it. No manner of resets, or punching the keyboard made any difference. Like many things in their tight, small, on-board world, they simply had to put up with it.

The Captain was on the flight deck when Star drew his attention to the screens. The battle fleet they were following was breaking its flight formation. On the screen the series of white flashing blobs suddenly burst out in all directions. Star pointed out a small planet.

"They're surrounding that planet." He pointed out.

The Captain looked closer at the screen and noticed that some of the dots were continuing the original direction.

"Battleships?" He asked.

Star nodded sending his double chins wobbling. "With fighter support. Whoever they are they seem to be aiming for that planet."

"Any idea who they are or what the planet is?" The Captain asked.

Edith pushed a button and the computer began to speak. Then she punched the consul and it fell silent. A sheet of paper slid out of a little gap. The Captain looked up. "

How did you do that?" he asked his engineering officer.

Edith just shrugged."The first law of Murphy's Theory of Mechanical Breakdown!"

The Captain nodded. "Hit it with a hammer?"

Edith smiled. "Something like that!"

He looked down at the paper. It told him that the planet was a mining outpost belonging to the Stella Knights. The ships were identified as belonging to The Dominion of Dave.

He looked up at Edith. "They are going to attack aren't they?"

Stars voice came from the navigation pod. "It looks that way. The fighters have formed a circle around the planet. It seems they are waiting for the battleships to get into position.

"Any sign of any thing happening down on the planet?"

Star punched some buttons and coordinates on his keyboard, his mechanical, eight-fingered hand making easy work of the task. An image appeared on his screen. It was the face of a human being. A very attractive, female, scantily dressed human being.

"Help me!" It mouthed.

The three of them looked at the screen and then at each other.

Cat Face peered out of the weapons pod. "Is she talking to us?" He asked.

The Captain looked across to Star. "I take it the signal originated from the planet?"

Star nodded.

The Captain sighed."I was afraid of that!"

Star peered closer at his screens. "You'll never get near enough to land. You couldn't thread a needle through those fighters."

The Captain thought for a few seconds. "Tractor beam?" He asked.

Edith shook her head. "Out of range, we need to be closer."

"How much closer?" He asked.

"Half a day!" Star replied.

The Captain looked at the fat, green man-like thing. "Why do you insist on marking time and distance by days? There are no days or nights out here."

Star continue looking at his screen. "There are in my head!"

There really was no arguing with that logic. The Captain had no idea of which planet or universe Star originated from. The one rule of a pirate captain and his ship was "ask no questions". People, or things, chose to become pirates for their own reasons, mostly very complicated and illegal ones. It was better not to know. As long as they signed the accord and adhered to the pirate code, they were welcome on board. Anyway over the years the four of them had forged a tight unit. They worked well with each other and, more importantly, learnt to trust each other's skill and judgement. Of course that meant they also had to put up with each other's little anachronisms and odd habits. At least they all had their own cabins, their own little bit of space where they could indulge their habits in private.

"Full forward." The Captain said as he pushed the ships wheel forward.

"Invisibility screens still up?"

He got a nod from Cat Face who lowered himself back into full blown weapons mode. Once in position he flicked switches, zoomed in and out of on-screen images and examined a number of potential targets.

"Bring it on!" he said in what sounded like a low cat growl.

The Captain glanced at Edith. She was tapping gauges and adjusting knobs and small levers on the central control desk.

She looked back at him. "All engines firing nicely. Just don't push the photon drive into the red. Too much red and they will explode!"

That wasn't the most comforting thing he'd ever heard. He liked running on red. Oh well, he pushed a button and the ship moved from one place to another.

"Beam in range!" She announced.

"Hit it!" The Captain ordered.

The cabin was filled with a loud buzzing. Then nothing. He looked around him.

"Did it work?" he asked.

Edith checked a screen. "Object aboard!" she said.

The Captain looked around the flight deck once again. "Where the hell is she then?"

Edith looked across the Star. "Just where were those co-ordinates targeted?"

Star checked his screens. "Down there on that planet, just where she was standing."

"I meant up here on the ship." Edith said patiently.

Star tapped the centre of his forehead with a blobby finger. "Ah. I see what you mean. The last time I use it was to lift that shipment of ice crystals from the hold of that Lucidian Trading Ship."

He looked up at The Captain. "She'll be in the main cargo hold."

Edith stamped out of the flight deck. "It's freezing in there, she'll catch her death in that skimpy outfit. I'll fetch her."

The automatic door made a slight hiss as it closed behind her. The Captain pushed the wheel forward again.

"Better get out of range!"

A few minutes later Star looked up from his screen. "Out of range, We've moved back half a day."

"Back to where we started!" The Captain remarked.

Star shook his head. "We can never go back to where we started. We may be near to where we started, but in a different place. The place where we started is ahead of us. It's where we would be if we weren't where we are now."

The Captain didn't even think about thinking about that one.

The door opened and Edith re-entered the flight deck. Behind her was a shuffling sound. She smiled at The Captain who was busy re-arranging his hair.

"I think you're in for a surprise!" She said and stood aside.

All eyes turned to the door. The shuffling sound grew louder and onto the flight deck came what could only be described as a very large fluffy penguin, only it couldn't be. Penguins didn't exist. They did once many, many, eons ago on a small blue planet in a parallel universe. They became extinct the same day the planet exploded. The captain tried to remember its name. Earth, that was it. He blinked.

"What are you?" Edith asked the penguin.

As she spoke the creature seemed to morph in front of their eyes. Now standing in front of them was the same shapely, half-undressed female they had seen on their screens.

The Captain scratched the back of his head and tried to hide his disappointment. "You're a shape shifter from the Nogee Galaxy aren't you!"

The half dressed attractive woman nodded. "I sure am. I ended up as a resource engineer working for the Stella Knights."

The Captain remembered the pirate code. He didn't ask any who's , why's or wherefores. In fact he didn't ask anything only...

"Why a giant fluffy penguin?"

The attractive half naked woman shrugged. "It was cold in the hold."

Star looked across at her. She looked back. "Are you a shape shifter too?" She asked.

Star gave a grunt and returned to staring at his screens. "No I always look like this!" He muttered.

The shape shifting woman had the decency to blush. Cat Face popped his head out of the weapons pod.

"What's going on in there?" he asked.

The woman glanced down at the cat face looking up at her. "It seems that the good folk of the Dominion of Dave have decided to have a border skirmish with the Stella Knights. The D & D claim the planet is theirs. The Knights have a different opinion. They won't attack, well not straight away. Those mines are a valuable resource. It's the only Nickelodium-Trioxide Mine this side of the galaxy."

As she spoke Star punched a button and a close-up image of the mining planet appeared on the main screen. A beam of light from a distant battleship hit its surface. There was a flash and an explosion. He turned towards the shape shifter.

"Has anyone told that battleship?"

The woman shook her head. "Probably just a warning shot. They want to attract attention!"

At that moment a flash occurred on the planet's surface and a circling fighter ship disappeared in a cloud of white heat.

"Just what the hell was that?" The Captain asked.

The woman shrugged. "The Knights have a full battle station down there, and when I say down there I mean down there. It's a mile underground. Any attacker would have to destroy the planet to eliminate it, and as I've already said, neither of them want that outcome. No planet, no Nickelodium Trioxide."

"So what happens now?" The Captain asked.

The woman moved towards him. He held up his hand. "I really would appreciate you putting some clothes on. It's distracting. In fact I think I preferred the Penguin persona. Better still why not revert to your natural shape."

The woman smiled. "You wouldn't want to see that!"

There was a slight popping noise and the penguin reappeared. The Captain let out a small sigh of relief. The penguin spoke, its voice was still that of the woman. It was all very wrong.

"The two sides will exchange fire. There will be casualties. Some of the miners have mates and young down there. The Knights have despatched their own battle fleet but it will take time to get here. The Leader down there thought diplomacy might prove a useful tactic."

A bad feeling began to grow in pit of The Captains stomach. He said nothing.

The penguin continued to talk. "Obviously the two sides cannot be seen talking directly with each other. Neither can either of them be seen to make the first move."

"So they need a go-between?" The Captain heard the words so he knew he'd said them, but he wished he hadn't.

The penguin nodded.

"Why me?" he asked.

The penguin tried to smile whilst the female voice

carried on speaking. "Because you were the only life force our scanners could locate."

The Captain turned and looked down at Cat Face. "I thought we had full screens engaged?"

Cat Face checked his switches and punched some buttons. "It seems to be working!"

The Captain gave him a look. "Are you sure?"

Cat Face pressed more buttons. "That's the problem with invisibility screens. You can never tell if they are actually there or not."

The Captain sighed and turned back to his visitor. "Why would the D & D listen to me?"

The penguin morphed once again. Now standing in front of The Captain was a humanoid shape with two arms and two legs, but with a face covered by some sort of striped mask. On its head was an ornate headdress. The Captain blinked.

"Because I will pass myself off as one of their own. We will trick them into believing I am a high ranking diplomatic counsellor from the Church of the Dominion of Dave and insist they allow my diplomatic mission to succeed."

The Captain tried, and failed, to stifle a slight giggle. "Won't they smell a rat? I mean just accidentally coming across one of their own counsellors out of the blue!"

The shape shifter gave a slight bow. "The counsellors from the Church of the Dominion of Dave hold great power. They carry much status and weight within their civilisation. They have freedom to roam, to preach and spread the word of Dave, they also undergo many diplomatic missions. The battle fleet commander will be surprised, he will be annoyed, but he won't question."

Cat Face shouted up from his weapons pod. "You mean a counsellor outranks a battle fleet commander?"

The replica D & D counsellor nodded. "Every time!"

The Captain turned to Star. "Hit the comms."

He might as well, after all the day couldn't get any stranger. He later came to regret that thought.

Buttons were pushed, screens flickered. Images came and went. Lines jumbled across the screen. It pixelated and then fragmented. Eventually the picture cleared. It showed the image of a humanoid dressed identically to the figure standing in front of him. He watched as the two figures bowed their heads to each other. The speaker gave a crackle and the man on the screen spoke.

"Counsellor, greetings in the name of Dave the Almighty, may his name always reign. We had no knowledge you were operating in this region."

The man in front of The Captain spoke. This time there was no trace of a female accent.

"And I you. I am engaged in a diplomatic mission to negotiate the purchase of Nickelodium-Trioxide. May I ask, with all inherent politeness, just what in the name of Dave the Almighty, may his name always reign, is your purpose is in attacking the mining planet in the middle of my mission?"

As he finished speaking he made a gesture of placing his left fist across his chest.

The humanoid figure on the screen bowed once again and repeated the hand gesture. "In the name of Dave Almighty, may his name always reign. We had no knowledge of such a mission. General Commander Advok ordered the assault himself."

The shape shifter made another gesture with his arm. The Captain thought it looked vaguely rude, but who was he to know about these people, or creatures, or whatever they were. An hour ago he had never heard of any of them. An hour ago he had been reasonably happy. Now life seemed complicated. He looked longingly at the lever controlling the photon drive. Then he thought better of it. If the D & D warlord thought he'd kidnapped a D & D councillor things could get awkward. He returned to the present. The man in front of him was speaking.

"Typical. Once again the Military and Priesthood have failed to communicate. This will take a deal of re-negotiation. My work has been made almost invalid. I am displeased."

The man on the screen bowed his head. There was silence. Then he looked back at the screen. "I will have to consult with my superiors. Please allow me time to make the necessary arrangements. My fleet will remain in position but we will not attack until the position has been clarified!"

The screen filled with horizontal lines and then fell dead.

The Captain looked at the shape shifter in front of

him. It had now changed once again. This time he appeared as a male humanoid with two arms and two legs and coloured blue.

"What now?" He asked.

The Blue Man shrugged. "We've probably the best part of two moons. His report will be passed to the General, who'll have to pass it up to his superiors, and they'll have to pass it up to someone at High Command who will have to verify the details with the representatives of the Counsellors. Then it will get passed upwards again. Eventually it will reach someone who will have to something about it. Then they'll contact the military and the priesthood and then we will be in very deep trouble."

"Two moons?" Asked the Captain.

"Thirty six hours!" Star said, not bothering to look up from his screens.

"Well that's alright then!" Edith added.

The Captain glanced at her. The android had seemed to master the art of sarcasm, or was it irony? It was difficult to tell with an android.

He jumped at the metal rasping noise behind him. He turned. It was just Star replacing his metal hand. He was replacing the five fingered type with the more powerful eight fingered variety. He saw the Captain watching.

"Could be some difficult co-ordinates to enter in!" He said as he wiggled all eight fingers at The Captain.

The Captain turned his attention back to the shape shifter, he had remained in the shape of the Blue Man. "So you have bought yourself some time. That's good. What do you intend to do with it?"

The Blue Man looked at The Captain. "I have an idea!"

"Thought you might!" Edith remarked.

Again The Captain wondered if she was being sarcastic or ironic or if she knew the difference between the two. He wasn't sure if he did. He turned his concentration back to what the Blue Man was saying.

"You pretend to be a Nickelodium-Trioxide merchant from somewhere far enough away to sound feasible. Tell the D&D that as there is some sort of property dispute, you are willing to pay them a large sum equal to the sum you are paying the Knights. I will authorise it."

The Captain thought for a few minutes as he tried to work out the chances of it going either wrong, or very wrong. "What about when they discover there is no payment?" He asked

The Blue Man smiled. "That is the beauty of my plan. The D&D are a bureaucratic race. By the time the requests have reached someone high up capable of making a decision the fleet will have gone away, or at least retreated."

The Captain nodded and then shook his head. "But eventually they'll want payment. What happens then?"

The Blue Man kept smiling. "By the time they discover there is no payment we will be gone!"

The Captain sighed and wondered if the Blue Man was deliberately being obtuse. He tried again.

"But when they discover they've been duped they'll be back, probably with a bigger fleet."

The Blue Man looked at The Captain wondering if

he was being deliberately obtuse.

"Like I said, we won't be there!"

The Captain sighed again. The conversation was going round in circles.

Edith spoke up. "When you say "we won't be there", who exactly do you mean?"

The Blue Man turned to her. "The mines, the miners, their mates and children, the whole thing, the planet!"

The Captain blinked. "The planet won't be there?" he asked incredulously.

The Blue Man nodded. "The Knights foresaw that owing a valuable resource could prove problematic. Mainly that other races would like to get their hands on it. So, when they constructed the mines they place a giant photon drive in its centre. As soon as the D & D battle fleet is out of the way, whoosh, the planet, the mines, everything flies off to another sector, equally far away from anywhere. "

As The Captain stood taking all this in, Cat Face popped his head out from the weapons pod.

"Do you mean the entire planet is actually a space ship?"

The Blue Man nodded.

"Cool!" Said Cat Face and slid back into his pod.

"Right then, get your tractor beam ready. We are about to go visit an Admiral of the Dominion of Dave in his battleship."

As the words left his lips the Blue Man changed shape once again the Captain found himself standing in front of a Counsellor of the Dominion of Dave.

Arranging the tractor beam took longer than anticipate, mainly due to the fact that they had used it once to bring up the shape shifting damsel in distress and they had to wait for its circuits and moving bits to cool down before it could be used again. As Edith pointed out, The Captain had said the model with the automatic cooling system was considered to be too expensive at the time, another hundred credits at least. She distinctly remembered The Captains comment "When do we ever need to use it twice in a row?" That had sealed the issue. She gave the cooling machine a kick. It didn't speed things up but it made her feel better.

Eventually the machine achieved the right temperature inter-balance. They were ready. The Blue Man turned to The Captain. "Aren't you going to change for the occasion?"

The Captain blinked. "I'm not a shape changer!"

The Blue Man looked him up and down. "I meant into something more befitting someone who's willing to spend about three million universal credits on a shipment of Nickelodium-Trioxide. Trust me, even small time Nickelodium-Trioxide dealers dress smarter than that!"

The Captain looked down at his tunic. It did look a bit grubby. He brushed at a small stain from a meal he didn't remember eating and then looked back at the shape changer.

"I'm not sure I've anything that's suitable!" he said.

Cat Face slid out of his pod. "I've a decent suit in my cabin. Picked it up when we robbed that space shuttle in sector eight. You remember it was when we....."

"It was meant to be carrying Lithium Crystals!" Edith snorted cutting him off mid sentence.

"It was the wrong ship!" Star added.

"It was a shipment of designer clothes heading towards a fashion week show on Nebulous Cludio." Cat Face said.

Fifteen minutes later The Captain found himself dressed in what seemed to be a purple velvet, wide lapelled suite. He looked down at his legs, he wasn't sure about the thigh boots. Edith gave his hair a final comb and pronounced him ready. He took another look at the thigh boots. He still wasn't convinced.

"How do I look?" he asked.

Cat Face gave him a glance. "Now I've seen it on, for the life of me I've no idea why I thought it stealing it was a good idea!"

"It's time!" The shape changing Counsellor said.

Buttons were pushed, calibrations made, little levers pulled. A couple of lights flashed on the control panel and the flight deck was suddenly two people less.

The three remaining crew members looked at each other. "Do you think he'll be believed?" Star asked.

"Only if they like purple!" replied Edith.

The Captain hated teleporting. He found being dissembled into a binary molecular structure and blasted across light years of empty space vacuum by a cheap tractor beam not only disconcerting, but it gave him a headache. He closed his eyes.

When he opened them again he was in a large white featureless room. He turned, the shape shifter was standing next to him head bowed. A panel in the wall opposite slid open and a bright light silhouetted the shape of the figure he has seen on the screen. The shape shifter was the first to speak.

"Greetings in the name of Dave Almighty, may his name always reign." As he spoke he struck his chest with his fist.

The newcomer lowered his head and repeated the gesture. "In the name of Dave Almighty, may his name always reign!" It said and then looked at The Captain. "Is this the merchant you speak of?"

The shape changer nodded and gave The Captain a quick nudge in the ribs. He stepped forward.

"I am authorised by my clients to negotiate a large shipment of Nickelodium-Trioxide." He bowed.

The Commander of the Battlefleet held his hand up for silence and turned to the shape shifter. "I do not understand why you are helping the Stellar Knights, our enemies." He remarked.

The shape shifter returned the salute "Diplomacy." He said.

The Commander shook his head. "I do not understand diplomacy. Sometimes the Council exceed their allotted remit!"

The shape shifter made a second gesture. "And would you defy the Will of Dave?"

That comment didn't seem to elicit the expected response. The Commander suddenly drew what appeared to be a large gun from his belt and held it in the direction of the shaper shifter who had already raised both hands into the air.

"I advise you in the name of the Council and Dave the Almighty to be very careful. Even as we speak our conversation is being transmitted to our Father Chapel within the Great Council."

The Commander glanced quickly around the room.

The shape shifter spoke again. "The transmitter is in

my eye. It is well said that Councillors of Dave are far seeing!"

The Commander snorted. "I will contact my superiors. There will be repercussions!"

"Of course it is within my power to make sure that half the payment is re-directed to the military. I will place the amount in universal credits directly into your personal account, purely for safe keeping of course!" The shape shifter added.

The Commander made another gesture with his arm across his chest. "That would be appreciated. May the Power of Dave be forthcoming!"

The shape shifter made another salute like gesture. "Forthcoming and more. There is just one thing else I request. The Knights will not be convinced of my impartiality if your fleet remains in position. They will see it for what it is, a threat of hostile action. It would ease my position if you could withdraw, just until the orders are confirmed, of course."

The Commander gave a snarl. "You ask too much Counsellor!"

The shape shifter bowed. "I ask in the name if Dave

the Almighty, may his name ever reign. I ask so His will be done."

The Commander of the battleship of the Dominion of Dave did not look pleased. He stared at the shape shifter. "May I remind you I am a Commander of the Battlefleet. I am not subservient to your commands!"

He took a step forward. As he moved The Captain noticed his finger had ever so slightly tightened on the trigger of his gun. He sniffed. There was a sudden smell of rat in the room and The Captain realised it had reached the nostrils of the D & D Commander, if indeed he did have nostrils under the face mask. One reason The Captain had survived out in the space lanes was he had a sixth sense for trouble. Another reason was his firm belief in the old adage "run away to fight another day". He pressed the button on his belt and felt the world around him melt.

When he opened his eyes he was back on his own flight deck. Standing in front of him were two men dressed alike. The shape shifter and the Commander of the D & D battle fleet. As he raised his gun there was a loud click and a voice spoke.

"The sound you just heard was the click of a safety

release. It belongs to a high impact XPC photon blaster. It will dissemble you and shoot your particles to all five corners of the known universe in a micro second!"

The Captain looked at Cat Face who was holding a hand gun. He was lying. It wasn't the high impact model but he didn't think it appropriate to mention it just now. He looked across at the shape shifter. The man was still using the shape of the D & D counsellor.

The shape shifter looked at the Commander. "Now I'm sure you wouldn't like your superiors to think you are so dull witted enough to allow yourself to be captured by a simple and very small band of space pirates, would you. I suggest you get on your communications and signal your fleet to withdraw."

The Captain wasn't sure if the shape shifter was being ironic or insulting. Before he could make a comment there was a dull thud and the shape shifter sank to his knees. As he fell he altered shape. By the time he was laying on the floor he had transformed into a large green slug. Standing over it with a spanner in her hand was Edith.

"I take exception to being called simple!" She said.

The Captain looked at the battleship commander. "He did have a point. Tell your fleet to withdraw!"

The Commander gave what could only be called a sneer coupled with a snarl. Then he punched his chest. There was a bit of sparkle and he disappeared.

"Bugger!" Said The Captain.

He turned to his controls. "We'd better get out of here, as soon as he's back on board, every gun on that battle ship will have us in its sights."

Star paused from his frantic button pushing. "No it won't! They'll do nothing."

The Captain turned towards him. "How do you figure that?"

Star grinned. "Because the Commander used his own device but jumped our tractor beam. He made the mistake of assuming it was still on its last setting. He thought he'd reappear on his own ship."

"And he hasn't?" Asked Edith, still standing over the inert form of the green slug.

"I tweeked it a bit. I flipped it back to a previous

setting!" Star said.

Cat Face was still standing, pointing a gun at where the D & D Commander had been. He grinned. "Nice!"

The Captain looked down at the gun. "I think we can put that away now."

He looked across to Star. "Just where is the Commander now?"

Stars flabby smile grew wider. "Down in the centre of the mining planet, where we picked the shape shifter up from. He's hardly likely to call down his own battlefleet when he's standing in the middle of the target. I have a feeling that the Stella Knights might have something to say about that!"

Edith smiled. "That is going to take a bit of explanation!"

"They'll probably hold him to ransom!" Cat Face said.

"As soon as he realises where he is he'll use the tractor beam to get back to his own ship." The Captain said as he began moving levers.

"He can't. Remember he used our beam? Well it's overheated again. It won't be useable for at least half a day."

Star bent over and blew on a switch. Then he looked back at The Captain. "That was meant to be an ironic gesture!"

The Captain checked some dials. "Let's get out of here. I'm not sure if I want to know what happens next."

Edith gave another swing with her spanner. "What about the slug here?"

"Put him in a secure box inside the hold." The Captain said as he pressed a button and flicked a couple of switches. Then they were somewhere else.

It was two days later when the shape shifter came around. At least The Captain assumed he was coming round. He'd never heard a slug groan before. He watched as two eyes on stalks peered around to discover where it was. It discovered it was in a cage inside a cargo hold. There was a plopping sound and the shape shifter returned to the form of the Blue Man. He rubbed the back of his head.

"What hit me?"

"Edith!" replied The Captain.

The Blue Man nodded, then wished he hadn't. He seemed deflated. "I suppose you'll be sending me back to the Nickelodium-Trioxide mines."

The Captain gave a slight, nervous cough. "We have a slight problem there."

The Blue Man looked up at hum. "What sort of problem?"

The Captain looked sheepish. "The tractor beam overheated and we had to leave."

The Blue Man cocked his head. "What happened to the battle fleet commander?"

"That's why the tractor beam was over heated."

"You sent him back to his ship?" The Blue Man said. Alarm showed on his face and he nervously looked around him half expecting to be blown out of space as he spoke.

The Captain shook his head. "No we sent him down the mine. He's hardly liable to order its destruction when he's standing in the middle of it."

The Blue Man sat and pondered this news for a moment and looked at The Captain. "It should lead to some interesting discussions. It might even start them discovering diplomacy for themselves!"

He then stopped speaking and thought in silence for a full minute. "You said "so we left". Left where?"

The Captain shrugged, "Wherever we were."

The Blue Man looked straight into The Captain's face. "You've kidnapped me!"

The Captain smiled. "Let's just say we're giving you a lift."

"But I never asked for a lift."

"Well then, you stowed away!"

The Blue Man looked around. "If I wanted to stowaway I'd have jumped a transporter, a fighter, anything but this second-hand bit of pirate space junk."

The Captain stood up. He was offended. "It might be second hand but it's not space junk. It's functional. I'll admit it has a few quirks. Anyway we like it!"

"There's room for improvement!" The Blue Man said after a slight pause as he waited for The Captain to sit down again.

As he sat The Captain glanced around the hold and did admit to himself it could do with a lick of paint. He let out a sigh. "It costs credits to upgrade ships!" he said quietly.

"Pirate business not doing too well then?" The Blue Man asked.

The Captain shrugged. "It has its ups and downs!"

"More downs than ups?"

The Captain just shrugged.

"I have an idea!" The Blue Man announced.
The Captain listened.

After the Blue Man had explained it The Captain stood up and returned to the flight deck.

"Has he come too yet?" Edith asked.

The Captain nodded.

"What are we going to do with him?" Star asked.

"That's why we need a ships meeting. We need to discuss the accord."

They all turned to look at him, even Cat Face stuck his head out of the weapons pod.

"The accord?" he asked.

The Captain nodded, "He's asked to join us. He wants to be a pirate!"

There was a general sound of groaning from everyone.

The discussion lasted the best part of a day. Slowly and methodically they weighed up the pros and cons. The main sticking point came when it was realised that it was a lot easier to divide things into four than it was to divide them into five. Star eventually pointed out that he could create a program that would calculate a fifth of anything. An argument then broke out when Edith pointed out that she had a calculator that could determine a fifth to one thousand decimal points. She didn't improve things when she added that a calculator had been around since time began. Cat Face just made things worse by asking when that was, who actually realised that time had actually begun, and what did they do before they realised that time was running, and when would it run out?

"Why don't we ask him why he wants to be a pirate?" Star asked.

Ten minutes later they were all in the hold looking into the cage. A degree of shock appeared on all four of their faces. Inside the cage was a full blown pirate. Not a space pirate but a seafaring pirate of ancient legend. On its face it wore an eye patch and a long black beard. On its head was a tricorn hat under which long, beaded strands of black hair fell to the shoulders. It wore a long frock coat with faded gold braiding under which was a waistcoat and white blouse. Around its waist was a thick leather belt into which was tucked a deadly series of knives, daggers, swords and cutlasses. Three pistols were stuffed into the waistcoat. There was a parrot sat on its shoulder.

"I think the peg leg might be a step too far!" Edith said.

The Captain glanced at her. Sarcasm or irony?

They sat down and began to discuss the accord. Eventually all questions were answered and all avenues explored and agreed upon. Then they signed it, but only after having to place a healing patch onto The Blue Mans hand where, in an act of misguided enthusiasm, he had cut himself and sent blood all over the document. Cat Face then pointed out they signed documents with ink and not blood.

Now the crew of Orcas Teeth was five. A sensitive, an android, a trigger happy cat, and now a shape shifter, all led by a man who was only human, in both good and bad ways, but mainly good.

It took a few days before The Blue Man, as he was now officially called, refined his pirate outfit. He ditched the cutlass and swords when he left the cage and attempted to climb the stairs out of the hold. Not only did they trip him up but he managed to discharge one of the pistols causing a large wooden chip to fly out of his wooden leg. The stuffed parrot kept falling off his shoulder, that soon disappeared. Eventually he settled on the blouse, the baggy trousers, the sea boots and the hair cut. He was in two minds about the wooden leg. Some days he wore one and some days he didn't. Eventually his mind was made up for him by the rest of the crew who told him they were fed up of the clumping noise it made as he limped along on the flight deck.

Chapter Two

They had drifted aimlessly for a few days when Star picked up some sort of signal. He turned to his keyboards and screens. Star maps and dotted lines appeared and then disappeared to be replaced by others. Eventually he lifted his head.

"Transporter Fleet!" he said.

The Captain gave the order. "Invisibility screens up!"

Down in the weapons pod buttons were pressed.

"Any idea who it belongs to and what it's carrying?" The Captain asked.

Star pushed more buttons and on screen images came and went.

"Silvainian Intergalactic Transport Corporation." He said.

"How do you know that?" The Blue Man asked.

"Because it's written on the side of the ships!" Star replied.

"Silvainian Intergalactic Transport Corporation. Better known as S.I.T. They operate in the Red Star sector. They claim to be the first choice in operational logistic." Edit shouted out. She was reading the information from a screen in front of her.

They looked at the ships on the screen. There were twelve of them, flying in a tight formation. The lettering on their sides could clearly be seen.

"Worth robbing?" Cat Face purred as he bunkered down in the weapons pod unclipping safety catches and flicking switches and looking at the screens in front of him.

"Someone thinks it is. They are being followed." Star said.

The Captain looked at the screen. "I can't see anything!"

"That's because you can't see it. It's screened. I'm a sensitive, I can see it." Star replied still looking at his screens.

Everyone else stared at the screen trying to see something that wasn't there.

"Coordinates?" Asked Cat Face.

Star punched some more buttons and numbers appeared on Cat Faces screen. Then Cat Face pushed some buttons.

"Target on!" He growled.

All eyes turned to the large screen. They watched for almost ten minutes before there was a bright flash and one of the transporters at the rear of the formation began to glow slightly and slow down.

"They are attacking!" Star said.

The Captain watched the screen carefully. The other transport ships continued on their route seemingly unaware of the fate of one of their number.

"They aren't taking evasive action!" he commented.

Star was busy punching buttons, his mechanical fingers working at double speed. Images came and gridlines flashed up on the screen to be replaced by others.

"No sentient beings on board. They are either flying on automatic settings or it's manned by droids." He added.

"In that case let's capture one for ourselves!" The Blue Man was beginning to get excited. This was what being a pirate was all about.

The Captain looked across at him and sighed. He hated enthusiasm. "Patience. I have a feeling that the SIT Corps don't let their ships be taken that easily."

"They've left it behind! Look!" The Blue Man pointed at the screen they were already looking at.

Star peered closer at the screen. "The attacker is pulling alongside. We can't see it, but it's there sure enough. They'll have to drop the screens to engage and get aboard. Watch closely."

Everyone did. That's why, when the explosion happened, they were all temporarily blinded. They all pulled back from the screen.

"What the hell was that?" The Blue Man shouted.

"They've blown up. The screens are blank, both ships gone." Star said, his voice shook slightly and his chins wobbled showing his shock.

"Far out!" Cat Face said. "That must have been some loaded device!"

The Captain looked across to Edith. "Get me all the available information on the SIT Corporation. I want to know why they would explode one of their loaded ships to prevent its capture!"

Edith began pushing buttons and peering at small screens.

The Captain looked across at Star. "Anything survive?"

Star shook his head causing his numerous chins to wobble even more. "Just a lot of space debris!"

"Any idea who the attacker might have been?"

Star made some adjustments to his mechanical hand and then looked down at his screens. "We may pick up some sort of clue among the debris, but I wouldn't hold your breath."

The Captain pushed a lever and the ship gave a slight forward lurch. "Let have a look at the debris!"

Star flexed his hand and began a series of complicated button pushing, the eight mechanical fingers flying over the keyboard.

"Going to be tricky. That transporter was large,

there's lots of moving bits and pieces out there."

The Captain leant forward towards the weapons pod. "Make sure all screens are up and functioning. Anything that comes near us, blow it up!"

"At the speed they are travelling small bits are just as dangerous as big bits." Edith said quietly.

"Vaporise it!" The Captain said.

Grinning, Cat Face engaged all shields and weapons. The Captain gave a little shudder. There was something about Cat Face's grin that unnerved him. It wasn't just the fangs. It was the look of sheer manic pleasure in his eyes. The only thing Cat Face liked better than polishing his weapons was firing them.

Whilst The Captain steered the ship through the debris causing it to sway and swerve, Star analysed everything that appeared on his screens. Suddenly he shouted the ages long warning.

"Whoa! Large shape appearing on starboard bow, I'd take a guess it's part of the transporters hull."

The Captain manoeuvred closer until its image filled the screens. Star was right. It was the remains of the transporters hull, an enormous framework of metal on which some outer cladding still remained. They could make out where the three decked cargo holds had been. At one end of the debris hung the remains of a control pod.

"Zoom in!" The Captain said.

As they watched the screen filled up with a tight close-up of the control pod.

"Anyone spot the anomaly?" The Captain asked.

"No central controls!" Edith observed.

"It's a droid ship!" Star remarked.

The Blue Man looked at The Captain with a question on his lips.

"No crew! Programmed to blow up on any alien contact!" The Captain explained.

"Alien contact?"

"Alien, as in anything or anybody that isn't an employee of the SIT." Replied Edith.

"Are all the transporters droid ships?" Asked Cat Face.

"Probably!" Replied Star. "The rest of the fleet is flying straight on as if nothing has happened."

"Someone, somewhere will know. The SIT pride themselves on their security." Edith commented.

"Can you track any communications?" The Captain asked.

Star wobbled his head. "No chance. Even if we picked up a signal it'll be encoded."

The Captain looked at Star. "How about checking the recording from earlier, before it blew up? I want to know if the transporter was the last one in the formation."

There was the sound of many buttons being pressed. "On screen now!" Star said.

They all examined the images. The attack had happened as the ship lagged behind the rest of the fleet.

The Captain looked around the flight deck. "Tell me where I'm wrong. The SIT convoy knew it was being tracked. One ship in the convoy was a decoy. As soon as the attackers were spotted the decoy ship falls back. It drew the attacker to it then, as soon as an approach was made, they blow the ship up taking the attacker out of the picture and allowing the rest of the fleet to continue unscathed."

The Blue Man nodded. "It makes sense. How many decoy ships do you think they have?"

The Captain shrugged. "Probably one per fleet."

The Blue Man smiled. "Just the one?"

The same thought crossed everyone's mind at the same time. The Captain looked across to Star.

"Are you sure they are all droid ships?" he asked. Star nodded. "Not a sentient being on board any of them."

Edith looked at her screen. "What's to say they are not protected by armed droids?"

Star made a little sucking sound with his mouth. "They could be!"

The Captain was standing behind the ships wheel looking at the image of the transporter fleet continuing on its way.

"How sensitive do you think its sensors are?"

"Very!" answered Star, "They picked up a ship that was shielded so well that I never saw it on my screen. I only saw it because I'm a sensitive. If they can pick that up they'll certainly pick us up as soon as we get inside their range."

The Captain remained silent. He was thinking. Everyone else remained quiet. Eventually he spoke.

"Let's just have a closer look at the wreckage. It might just tell us something about the ships we don't know."

An hour later they were drifting between two large pieces of wreckage when there was a bump. At first it was a little bump, just enough to cause the ship to lurch a little. Then there was a ripping sound.

"We've run into something!" Cat Face shouted from the weapons pod.

"You were meant to vaporise anything that came near us!" The Captain shouted back.

The voice came back "Didn't see anything."

The Captain looked across to Star who shrugged his shoulders and set his body off on another wobble. He peered closer at his screen and then suddenly slapped his forehead with his non metallic hand.

"The ship was in invisible mode. Stands to reason its debris must still be in that state!"

The Captain was about to say something but was interrupted by a sudden judder. Edith pushed some buttons and looked at her screen then she pushed some more buttons. "Power loss on the sub-proton drive. We've taken damage."

She pressed more buttons and checked another screen. "The ships support systems have been damaged!"

As if to prove her point the lights flickered and dimmed. Edith looked up at the dimmed light.

"The air conditioning is on the same circuit. I don't want to worry anyone unduly, but if my calculations are right, we have a day to find and fix the problem. Then we run out of air."

"That's useful," The Captain commented."Do you think you can sort it in time?"

"It's not useful at all, and I'm not certain I can fix it in time. I think the damage is mechanical and if we haven't got the spares...."

Edith shrugged and let her words trail off. Then she bent down and opened a trap door in the floor of the flight deck that led to the ships engines and workings. The Captain pulled the power and let the ship go into drift mode as Edith lowered herself down and disappeared from view without completing her sentence.

As Edith worked below them the rest of the crew sat at their stations. Star stared at the screens trying to identify invisible bits of wreckage. Cat Face locked and unlocked the safety catches on his weapons. The Blue Man looked at The Captain.

"Shouldn't we be doing anything?"

The Captain looked at him. "We are, we are conserving air!"

The Blue Man took the hint and shut up.

An hour and a half later Edith popped her head out of the trap door.

"You don't happen to have a replacement titanium

drive shaft and two irithium gaskets on board by any chance?"

The Captain shook his head. Edith disappeared again.

An hour later her head reappeared once more. "How about a lithium directional interchanger?"

The Captain shook his head once more. This time Edith didn't disappear. Instead she lifted herself out of the trapdoor back onto the flight deck. She didn't say anything.

After a while The Captain looked across at her.

"Anything else we need?"

She turned towards him. "A few bits and pieces wouldn't go amiss."

He nodded. "Make a list!" he said.

The Blue Man decided to risk using up some air to ask a question. "Why are you making a list? If we haven't got it we haven't got it. You can't conjure stuff out of thin air!"

The Captain looked at him. "Actually I can!" he said.

The Blue Man froze. "How?"

The Captain nodded towards the screen. "There must be a dozen of what we need out there, all we have to do is steal it!"

As his words sunk in here was a small purring sound coming from the weapons pod. Edith leant over her consul. "I'll make a list, complete with specs and illustrations. I don't want you bringing back the wrong items!"

"Just how do you propose stealing something from that transporter fleet? They'll see you coming."

The Captain looked at Star. "Can you get us within tractor beam range?"

Star nodded.

The Blue Man looked at The Captain. "You mean you're going to teleport yourself onto one of those transporters?"

The Captain shook his head and The Blue Man gave out a short sigh of relief.

"We are going to teleport onto one of those transporters!"

Before the Blue Man could say anything else The Captain continued.

"It makes sense. You can shape shift to one of their droids. Scout it out for us and we'll do a bit of light fingered, reverse engineering."

The Blue Man leant on the bulkhead wall of the flight deck and remembered working in the mines. He was happy there.

Star managed to navigate a course through the debris. He scanned his screens. Bright red dots pulsated and moved, they represented the remains of the two ships. With luck the debris might confuse the automatic sensors on the SIT transporters. If so they stood a chance of getting through.

The Blue Man turned to Edith. "I don't suppose you could track down an image of a SIT Corporation droid. It helps to know what it is I'm meant to be shape shifting into!"

It was half a day later when Star looked up from his screens. "We are within range of the tractor beam."

He announced and then added, "Well as near as I can get!"

The Captain moved from his position on the wheel. Edith took over as Cat Face climbed out of the weapons pod. He was armed to the teeth with various pistols and laser blasters strapped to his body. He opened up a small cupboard and pulled out a handful of small stun grenades. He grinned as he put them into various pockets in his suite.

The Blue Man had done what all shape shifters do. He had shifted his shape. Now standing between Cat Face and The Captain was a large, upright, metallic oval, not too dissimilar to a large and thin egg. Lights blinked on and off and a number of tubes and attachments suggested it was armed.

The Captain scanned the image of the transporter ship on the screen in front of him. "Send us to the ship in the centre of the formation. They won't risk blowing that one up. Keep an eye on it though. If it begins to drop back or move out of formation hit the beam and bring us back. No hesitation!"

Star nodded and pressed a switch. Three people weren't on the flight deck anymore. He looked across towards Edith. "How long before the systems begin to fail?"

Edith glanced at her screen. "A day, give or take a couple of hours."

Chapter Three

When they opened their eyes the three of them
found themselves inside a large open space. The
Captain looked around. The light was dim but he
could make out he was standing at the edge of a
large storage area, big enough to house his ship
twice over. He listened. There was an overbearing
silence broken only by the distant throbbing of
engines and the humming of systems working away.
He consulted the diagram of the ships interior that
Edith had created. She had also downloaded all
available data on the SIT Corps and its transporter
fleets. That information was now in a chip inserted
into the back of The Captains eye patch that was in
fact, a small screen that projected its images directly
into The Captains unseeing retina, and from there,
directly into his brain.

"It's just like seeing things!" he said when it was
first implanted.

"It is seeing things!" was the reply.

Cat Face held a large hand blaster and gently
swayed it one way and another, peering into the
dark, unlit areas. Next to them hovered a battle
droid. The Blue Man had made his transition. The

Captain nudged the droid and pointed towards the far end of the storage area. According to his information there should be doorway that led onto some sort of engine room where, hopefully, he would find the bits and pieces listed on Edith's "shopping list".

They moved quietly with the droid taking the lead. They found the door, it was automatic and opened with a slight mechanical hiss. The Captain peered down what appeared to be a long corridor. He closed his one good eye and allowed the eye patch to project the plans of the ship into his brain. He opened his good eye again and focused as the two images superimposed themselves. When the two images met he noticed that Edith had drawn a large red arrow with the words "In here!" written against it.

He followed the arrow down the corridor to another door which led to another, shorter corridor. They followed it until they came to a large sealed double door. The Captain nodded towards the droid who propelled itself to the front of the door where it was suddenly bathed in a bright blue light.

Cat Face held his gun at the ready. "Intel scan!" he muttered.

They braced themselves, waiting for the scanner to sound the alarm. It didn't. Instead there was a hum and the doors slid open. As they opened they revealed an engine room.

It took the best part of an hour for The Captain to identify the parts he required, and the best part of a second hour to bypass and uncouple them. Once he had them out of the engine he placed them into the centre of the room and tapped some co-ordinates into a small consul on his wrist. A green light covered the stolen parts and they disappeared from sight. The Captain nodded. He was about to press the recall button for themselves when Cat Face tapped him on the arm.

"Let's go back to the storage hold!"

The Captain turned to him. "Why? We've got what we came for."

Cat Face smiled. It was his evil grin. "Why not take something else, something that might yield us a profit?"

The Captain thought for a second and then nodded his agreement. It made sense. At least he may be able to pay off some of his debts. The three of then turned around and returned the way they had come. The walk back to the hold proved uneventful.

As they re-entered the storage hold they looked around. It seemed very empty.

Cat Face turned to the Captain. "It's a transporter ship, so why is there no cargo?"

The Captain checked the ships plans once again.

"There's a second storage hold behind that bulkhead". He said.

They searched until they found a door. It opened. The shape shifting droid entered first with The Captain and Cat Face close behind. They emerged on a metal walkway high up on the side of this second hold. Then they looked down.

Below them was row after row of Battle Droids. They were silent all standing facing the same way. Cat Face nudged the Captain and pointed out two large Battle Tanks.

"Laser blasters, thermal missiles, and enough firepower to attack a small planet!" he whispered.

The three of them looked at each other and The

Captain nodded towards the door. Very quietly they left the balcony and closed the door behind them. The Captain pressed a button on his wrist and the three of them disappeared, their particles flashing along the tractor beam.

They re-emerged on the flight deck. Star looked up from his screens.

"Well that proved easy enough!" Then he noticed their faces. "What's the matter?"

"They are carrying a battle fleet!" The Captain said.

Star gave a little snort. "Can't be. It's a regular transporter route. SIT operate all across this sector. You've seen the company breakdown."

The Captain looked around. "Where's Edith?"

Star pointed to the open trapdoor. "She began fitting the replacements as soon as they materialised."

The Captain nodded. "That's good, very good. We just might need to get out of here fast!"

Star examined his screens. "There's nothing out there, just the transporters continuing their route like nothing's happened."

"Where are they heading?" Cat Face asked.

Star continued looking at the screens and moved his mechanical hand across a number of keyboards. Time passed, then some more time. Eventually he turned towards the flight deck. "Large screen!" he said.

They all looked up at the screen. It was showing an image of a large, free floating space station.

"Alpha XP!" he announced.

"How far away?" Asked The Captain.

"Six days!" Star replied.

The Captain continued staring at the image. "We need to get there in four!"

The Blue Man looked across the flight deck. "Why do we need to go there?" he asked.

"Because someone should let them know there's a droid army heading in their direction." The Captain replied.

It took the best part of a day for Edith to cannibalise and customise the damaged support systems.

Eventually she was satisfied that it was not only repaired, it was also updated and more efficient than it was before. Mind you, given the state of the ship, that didn't take much in the doing.

As Edith worked below the rest of the crew spent the time arguing the pros and cons of what they should and shouldn't do. The argument went as follows.

Why should they get involved in something that clearly wasn't their business?

If the battle fleet of droid warriors was heading in your direction wouldn't you appreciate someone telling you?

Are all the transporters carrying battle droids?

They couldn't answer that last question. They had estimated they had seen at least five hundred plus the two battle tanks. If each ship carried the same they were looking at an army of at least six thousand.

"Eleven!" Argued Cat Face. "Remember, one ship blew up!"

"Suppose their target isn't the space station?" The

Blue Man asked. "Perhaps it's just a refuelling stopover and their real target is somewhere else? Or perhaps they've already done their fighting somewhere else and are being returned home, wherever that may be!"

The Captain shook his head at the last idea."They were in A1 condition. No battle scars. They are on their way somewhere."

"A factory shipment?" Star suggested.

Everyone fell silent. As possibilities went it was as good as the others.

Then Edith poked her head out of the engineering trapdoor and climbed onto the flight deck. "Fixed!" She said wiping her hand on some sort of oily rag.

"As good as new?" Asked The Captain.

"Better!" She replied.

They abandoned the idea of moving ahead of the battle fleet when The Blue Man pointed out that if they went ahead, and the fleet attacked they would be putting themselves in the middle of the target, Instead they decide to shadow the fleet for the next few moons, just to see what happened.

They were a moon away from the space station when Star looked away from his screens and glanced towards the flight deck

"Picking up comms transmissions!" he announced and moved his hand across his keyboards.

"Patching in!" he said.

Everyone looked up at the large screen on the flight deck. At first it showed a lot of broken lines and then frozen pixilation's, then the image of a man in the uniform of the SIT. He was in the process of requesting permission to refuel. The images changed to that of the space stations reply. The screen fuzzed and cleared revealing a female face. She responded by suggesting the pilot take a holding orbit around the station and await further instructions. Everything seemed very ordinary.

The Captain punched some buttons of his own and brought the space station into view. Small craft flew in and out of the landing docks positioned around the massive structure. Large fuel tankers drifted out from the station to couple up with and fill up the ships held in orbit. Lights lit up the station so it looked like a Christmas tree.

The Captain glanced down at the weapons pod.

"Retract all shields!" He said.

The Blue Man looked across the flight deck at him.

"It's considered bad form to approach a service station with all shields up. It arouses suspicions."

The Captain said as he pointed towards the screen.

"That thing has more firepower than half dozen battle cruisers. Helps dissuade anyone from attempting to rob or attack it, or any other actions the owners disapprove of. The last thing any Captain needs on his approach is to arouse their suspicions."

Stars voice broke in. "Captain, there's movement on the transporter fleet."

Star switched the image on the screen to that of the transporter fleet. At first everything seemed normal. He punched a button and the image zoomed into one particular transporter. Its undercarriage was opening up. All eyes watched as hundreds of small egg shaped metallic objects began falling. As they dropped some sort of propulsion system kicked in. The Captain switched to a wider view. From the bottom of all the transporters hundreds of battle droids began to fly towards the space station.

They moved so fast that, by the time anyone on the station realise what was happening, the droids had landed on the structure and were blasting their way inside. A beam of white light suddenly burst from the space station and two transporter ships simply disappeared from sight, vaporised.

"Shields up!" The Captain said.

Cat Face grumbled from inside the weapons pod. "Up down, up down, make your mind up!"

The Captain turned to where the voice had come from. "I don't want some sharp shooter on the station to mistake us for part of the battle fleet."

In the time it took him to speak the words the guns of the space station were fully engaged. White lines of lethal energy burst in all directions, many hit the transporters. In less than a minute all of them simply ceased to exist. All over the station itself there were flashes of light and small explosions.

"They are inside!" The Captain stated the obvious.

As if to confirm his words a number of smaller ships began to emerge from the docking bays.

"Rats leaving a sinking ship!" Cat Face remarked,

"Given the choice I'd be with the rats any day!" The Blue Man remarked.

Before anyone could answer a series of beams flashed out of the station and a chain of explosions lit up their screens. When the light had died down there were no ships, just a lot of glowing space debris and wreckage floating about. Nobody said a word.

It didn't take long for the fighting on the space station to die down. The battle droids must have swept through the place killing anyone or anything that stood in their way. No ships attempted to leave. The Captain tried to count the number of ships that had attempted to escape as around twenty. There might be more inside, but after seeing what had happened to the others, no one seemed willing to take the gamble. He looked across at Star.

"Did they manage to get a distress signal off?" He asked.

Star shook his head. "Can't tell, there's so much jumble and static out there it's impossible to pick up any signals."

The Captain nodded and pressed a small lever forward. Suddenly the ship was a day away.

"What was all that about?" Edith asked.

"Unfriendly takeover?" The Blue Man offered.

The Captain shook his head. "Space stations are supposed to be safe places, sanctuaries, places outside regional disagreements and wars. There was the agreement signed years ago that granted them immunity and neutrality."

"So someone didn't read the small print!" Cat Face remarked.

"Clever trick though!" The Captain added. "Get in close undercover and stage a surprise attack!"

The Blue Man shook his head, "Too expensive. Those transports don't come cheap!"

Edith laughed. "That's the beauty of their plan. Those transporters weren't there's. They are the property of the SIT Organisation. They were hired to transport the battle droids."

The Blue Man smiled. "Someone at the SIT isn't going t be a happy chappie then. Once they find out what's happened they'll send a battle fleet to blow Alpha XP out of space!"

Edith shook her head. "That's why the plan was so subtle. The SIT are a bona fida company. They won't dare attack the station. It's against all galactic laws."

The Captain looked across towards Star. "How long do you think it will be before someone at SIT realises what's going on?"

Star shrugged. "It depends on how closely the SIT monitor their transporters. It might take them at least a moon to discover they don't exist anymore!"

The Captain smiled. "Let's tell them now. There could be a few credits in it!"

"Will they pay for bad news?" Edith asked.

"Course they will, why else do people subscribe to news casts?" Cat Face said. He was right.

It took Star the best part of an hour before he could make contact with anyone at the SIT head office that was in a position to do anything. They had spent the time being passed from one department to another, from person to android to person to the most infuriating muzak he had ever heard before a grey haired man appeared on the screen in front of him. He introduced himself.

"Luke Pearson, assistant head of security for the SIT organisation. I have no idea how you got patched into my comms but please make it brief. I have a busy day in front of me!"

Star punched a button and the screen split showing both Luke Pearson and The Captain. The Captain didn't bother with introductions.

"I have news concerning the fate of one of your transporter fleets."

Luke Pearson picked up on the use of the word "fate".

"All our fleets are fully accounted for!" He said brusquely.

"Does that include the one currently floating in bits around the Alpha XP space station?"

The grey haired man on the screen turned away and consulted someone out of vision. There was the sound of someone punching buttons and urgent whispers. The grey haired man turned back to the screen.

"We seem to have a communication problem with the fleet in question!" he said.

"That's because it isn't there anymore." The Captain remarked and looked across to Star. "We did record the visuals didn't we?"

Star nodded.

The Captain looked at the grey man. "Here's the deal. Before I tell you anything else I am transmitting an account number to you. I would like one thousand universal credits to be deposited into it via a non recoverable credit transfer."

The man in grey looked at the screen with the surprise of someone who has just been slapped across the face by a large wet fish. He blinked. He recognised blackmail when he saw it.

The Captain continued as if reading his thoughts. "Please do not mistake this as an attempt to blackmail you. It is purely a business transaction. I have the information you need. I need money and you are a multi billion credit company with more assets than some small galaxies. A thousand credits is fair exchange."

The grey haired man remained silent so The Captain continued. "Don't forget, it's accountable. Your people can claim tax on it and it won't affect any insurance claims you may wish to pursue."

Luke Pearson swallowed. "I do not have the authority to sign such a payment. I will have to consult my superiors."

The Captain gave a little sigh. "The news that you guys have lost an entire transporter fleet will travel around this galaxy quicker than any ship you send can get here. Even if I don't contact every news outlet I can find and sell them the footage there could well be survivors. They will tell anyone and everyone they meet what's happened here. I'll give it a moon before your share price begins to drop. Three moons before you lose every contract you have."

The man on the screen punched a few buttons. "The payment is on its way!"

The Captain looked across to Star who peered at a small screen and then nodded at The Captain.

"We're one thousand universal credits better off." He said.

The Captain looked at the screen and told his story, carefully missing out the bit about boarding one of their ships and stealing company equipment. When he had finished speaking a second face appeared on his screen. By the cut of his uniform and by the way he spoke they could all see he was someone very high up in the Corporation.

He introduced himself. "My name is Huddle. I'm the Director of SIT Security. I have been fully informed of the situation. I have a job for you!"

Everyone on the flight deck glanced at each other. The Captain looked back at the screen.

"Just what nature of commission would you be requesting of us?" He asked. He had a bad feeling, the type of feeling someone gets when they are about to be offered a large sum of money to do something they really didn't want to do, but can't afford to turn it down.

Huddle continued speaking. "I want you to find out who the attackers are, where they come from. Infiltrate the space station."

The Captain shook his head. "You're in a better position to do that. All you have to do is check your invoices. Find out who hired your fleet."

Huddle looked back at him without any expression on his face. "We already have. I do know my job Captain! According to our records we were transporting a batch of mining droids and mining equipment for a company that suddenly doesn't seem to exist anymore. They liquidated this morning. The data trail ends there."

The Captain shook his head. "So if you and your resources have come to a dead end what do you expect me to do and, more to the point, how?"

The Security Director smiled. It was an icy smile. "I'm sure you'll find a way. After all, you did manage to teleport aboard one of our transporters and steal our engine parts."

Everyone on the flight deck fell silent and looked at each other as the man on the screen continued to speak.

"Oh don't pretend you didn't. We checked the security footage that was beamed to us before the ship was destroyed and saw you creeping along one of the corridors. The engine sensors told us some interference had taken place. We ran some checks on you and your ship. Do you know there's a very large file dedicated to you and your crews exploits? It's held by most law enforcement agencies and security companies in this galaxy. The only reason you haven't been apprehended yet is that you are still rated as "low priority". That means no-one considers it worthwhile enough to chase you around the universe, that situation could change!"

He gave the crew sometime for that point to sink in and then added. "On the up side I have to compliment you on gaining access to our ship. Somehow you managed to evade all our shields and security devices, plus the fact that you're already in the location. That's why I'm offering you the job!"

The Captain looked at the screen. "A commission? How much are the SIT willing to pay for such, information?"

Huddle didn't even blink as he spoke. "Our commission will be for one hundred thousand universal credits!"

The Captain staggered and Edith had to step forward to prevent him from falling over. Out of the weapons pod a strange purring noise could be heard. The Blue Man mentally ran through the wording of the accord he had recently signed, a sixth to the ship and one sixth to each of the crew. That was the best part of sixteen thousand universal credits each, he smiled. Star said nothing but smiled as he continued to press various buttons and keyboards.

The Captain looked at the Director of Security. "Agreed!" he said.

Huddle punched a button off screen. "Contracts will be exchanged within the moon. I will advise my people to fix a permanent communications link with your comms station. From there I would appreciate a link into your eye-patch device. We're investing a deal of money in this venture. I want to make sure that investment is sound!"

The Captain considered this idea. On the one side, he didn't like the idea of anyone being inside his head, let alone the Director of SIT Security. On the other side, he wouldn't be alone. His would be a shared responsibility. He wouldn't have to solely carry the blame when everything went wrong, and it was a lot of money. It was a no brainer, or in this particular case, a two brainer. He nodded his agreement.

"I have a question!"

Everyone looked across the flight deck towards Star then his large, green, flabby face appeared on the screen.

Huddle looked at him. "So, you are the sensitive, the one with the mechanical hand."

Star lifted up his hand. It was the one fitted with eight fingers. He wriggled them at the screen as he asked his question. "I'd like to know how your transporter transmitted a request to refuel at the space station. I saw that signal, it was human to human. I was under the impression that your fleet was manned by androids."

The Director of Security shook his head. "There was no human on board the transporters. Strictly droid operated."

A coin of small denomination dropped at the back of The Captains mind. "Was the fleet scheduled to refuel at Alpha XP?"

The director shook his head. "The transporters carried enough fuel to complete the journey without the need to refuel."

"Where was their destination?" The Blue Man asked.

"Piper Down XPI, a small mining colony, five moons from the space station. Their course would pass near, but they would have no need to stop."

"I take it that...."

Huddle shook his head, cutting off The Captains question. "We've been in contact. No one in the colony ordered any droids."

The Captain sighed. "It seems whoever planned this attack managed to make some very large holes in your security."

Huddle shrugged. "We can't vet every order for every shipment. If the required data meets our security checks the orders are fulfilled."

Suddenly Cat Face appeared on the screen. "Someone's gone to a lot of trouble an expense just to capture a space station. What's the big deal about owning a space station?"

The Director of Security nodded. "That just might be the most important question of all. The hundred thousand universal credit question!"

An idea began to formulate in the back of The Captains mind. "I have the beginnings of an idea. I want to stand off for a little while. I want to watch what happens next."

"Why?" was the question fired back from the screen.

The Captain stared back and held up his hand, counting each point off on one of his fingers. "One, because I want to see if anyone turns up to claim the station from the droid army. Two, to see what happens when the next ship turns up looking to refuel, replenish and enjoy some R&R."

Edith's face suddenly appeared on the screen. "Why haven't you mentioned to us the fact that the SIT Organisation actually owns the space station? Oh, and don't say it's data claims it's an independent operation, but following the data tells me that it actually belongs to a subsidiary of a subsidiary of a company registered to the SIT!"

The comment had plainly touched a nerve. Huddles face grew severe. "That's another reason I need to find out who is behind this and why it has been captured. I will leave you to your observations, but I will be in constant contact!"

The screen went blank. The crew set to work. The Captain placed the ship in a wide orbit around the space station, far enough to be out of range of scans, but near enough for Star to track any of its communications.

Edith spent her time down in the trapdoor adjusting the flight controls, tweaking the repairs. After making sure all the screens were in place Cat Face adjusted the many weapon firing controls in front of him and made sure everything was fully loaded. Then they sat down and discussed what the hell they should do next.

Of course the word discuss doesn't really describe the arguments and various ideas and plans they all put forward. Eventually a consensus appeared. They would call and book themselves into the space station as if nothing has happened. Indeed all the signals and visual communications indicated that nothing had. The space station floated as normal with all its operating lights fully working. Star pointed out that all the debris from the destroyed transporter ships had somehow vanished from their screens. Finally it was a joint decision that they would wait until one or two other ships approached and landed, after all, as the Blue Man pointed out, the mission would soon come to an untimely end if the space station blew the first approaching ship out of existence, at least by waiting for others they would discover the type of reception awaiting any approaching ship.

A day later Star picked up a signal. "There's a ship approaching, small transporter. I've hacked into it. Switching on comms."

The screen flickered into life. They saw the image of a transporter captain and heard him request permission to land. The screen flickered and his image was joined by that of a woman traffic controller based on the space station. She acknowledged the request and designated the appropriate landing and boarding co-ordinates. Everything looked like business as usual.

Star turned towards The Captain. "I've checked. That was the same woman that permission to the SIT Transporter fleet."

The screen switched to the external view and they watched as the newcomer flew towards the space station and landed. Nothing happened. As they watched another ship came into range.

"Second ship approaching!" Star said.

Everyone watched. The procedure was exactly as it was before. Permission was requested and permission given. They watched as the ship approached and landed. Once again everything seemed normal.

"OK everybody. Our turn!"

The Captain manoeuvred the ships controls and it

slowly moved from its orbit onto a trajectory that aimed directly at the space station. Star pressed his buttons and transmitted the official requests to land. It was granted by the same woman as before. The Captain brought the ship safely into Dock Four. As they left the ship and entered the air lock the first thing they saw was a bar.

The Captain bought the first round and they found a table. Everything seemed normal. He bought a second round, which was unusual, then it was everyone for themselves. After four drinks the drinks turned from sensible beers to dubious cocktails. Cat Face looked down at the thing he had just ordered. It had arrived complete with a curly straw, bubbles and steam that oozed out from a purple and yellow concoction.

"Shouldn't at least one of us remain sober to keep an eye on things?" Edith asked.

The Captain nodded his agreement.

"Perhaps we should all take it easy on the alcohol." He murmured as he ordered another drink.

Edith sighed. Cat Face looked right and left to make sure no one else was in listening distance, there wasn't. He leant across the table. "This is normal.

Anyone docking into the station is bound to get drunk the first night. In fact their security might pick up on anyone who's just landed and doesn't get drunk!"

Edith acknowledged that he had a point and ordered herself another dubious cocktail. The evening came and went, ending by the crew of Orcas Teeth staggering, crawling and gibbering all the way back to their ship where they tried and failed to get themselves into their bunks. Edith made it. Cat Face fell asleep in his weapons pod. The Captain would have made it but he got himself trapped in his own automatic door and fell asleep half in and half out of his cabin.

Star and the Blue Man became absorbed in a discussion about the rules of the game of Neptunium Overball. As with all drunks they fell out before becoming bosom buddies. Eventually the alcohol affected Blue Mans shape shifting abilities and he suddenly and inexplicably changed into a potted palm. This confused Star, one minute he was talking to a blue man the next he was talking to a plant. His drunken mind decided that being seen talking to potted palm would probably bar him from getting another drink so he picked up the plant inside its pot and placed it in the corner of the room among other types of potted plants. Eventually he used his navigation skills to get back to the ship but lost his way in one of the corridors and ended up in the cargo hold where he promptly curled up and went to sleep.

Once the bar was empty and all the travellers safely back in their own ships, the lights went down and the bar closed. The staff tidied up the used glasses and polished the tables. Then one at a time they simply close down and froze. Even in his drunken state as a potted palm the realisation that the bar was staffed by androids sobered the Blue Man up. He stayed where he was. Almost an hour later the first battle droid hovered into view. Its weapons scanned the room and then it passed by. The potted palm stayed where it was. It needed to think about this new development.

The following morning wasn't good for any of them. The Captain had a monumental hangover and a bruised hip. Star had managed to get out of the hold and was in the medical bay desperately searching for anything that could take his headache away. Edith woke up, took her head off, made a few adjustments and put it back on. Clear headed she made her way to the flight deck where she eventually tracked down the strange buzzing noise to the weapons pod. It was Cat Face snoring.

Meanwhile in the bar the potted palm sat watching as a battle droid hovered at the doorway. A beam of light emanated from its top and the frozen figures came back to life and started to prepare the bar for another days drinking. Eventually it began to fill with people wanting food and drink. No one took a second glance at a Blue Man who ordered a breakfast bowl, ate it and left the bar.

Edith looked up as he entered the flight deck. "Rough night?" She asked.

"An interesting one!" Was his reply.

He looked around. "Where is everyone?"

"They are all sleeping it off. Star and The Captain are in their cabins and Cat Face is asleep in the weapons pod. That's the odd noise you can hear."

The Blue Man nodded. "I thought the air con was playing up. Better wake everyone up and tell them my news!"

Edith cocked her head to one side. "What news is that?"

"The station is patrolled by battle droids and all the staff have been replaced by androids!"

Edith said nothing but walked across to her consul and began pressing buttons and reading the lines and graphs that appeared on her screens. She examined the data and looked back at the Blue Man.

"You're right. According to this scan the only humans on board the station are outcomers. No human staff register on these scans."

The Blue Man shook his head. "It doesn't make any sense. Why take over a service station? They can't make all that profit."

Edith pressed a small yellow button. In the distance a siren could be heard. In a few minutes The Captain appeared on the flight deck. He was dishevelled and looked like he'd just been running.

Before he could say anything Edith spoke. "Better get in touch with Huddle. We've got some news for him!"

The Captain was about to reach for his comms when a very green looking Star wobbled onto the flight deck.

"Don't do that! If they have taken over the station they'll probably be monitoring all transmissions out of here."

The Blue Man looked at him. "How do you know? You weren't in the room when I spoke."

Star spoke as he moved across to his comms and navigation station. "I'm a sensitive. Remember?"

The Captain stood at his controls and flicked a few switches. "Take us back to our original orbit."

Star punched some buttons and The Captain pushed the wheel forward. The ship slowly moved out of the station and into space. As it moved away from the station he punched another button. Suddenly the ship was somewhere else.

As soon as he determined they were well out of range of the station The Captain made contact with Security Chief Huddle. As he updated him Star kept an eye on the screen showing the space station. Everything seemed normal, ships came and went, however he did pick up the traces of a very faint signal surrounding the station. He was right. Every transmission in and out of the place was being scanned and monitored. He tried to smile but his head still hurt too much. He turned his attention to The Captains conversation.

Huddle was patiently describing to the rest of the crew that all SIT personal on board the space station were androids and that no, it wasn't common knowledge. Over the years the management had realised that serving drinks, patching up damaged ships, cleaning rooms, providing storage and manning gambling tables on a station at the far end of a non-too populated galaxy didn't tick all the boxes that said job satisfaction. Not only did they find it difficult to recruit staff, but the staff they did recruit were not the finest minds in the galaxy. Many of them tended to have a reason for hiding away in the back of beyond. Others fell prone to space fever and had to be shipped out. Androids did the job better, without complaining. What did concern him was that the company's androids seemed to accept the presences of the battle droids. He was also able to confirm that no communication was recorded prior to the invasion.

Star looked up from his consol. "I assume you have full visual communications with the station?"

The Head of Security nodded once. "Reports from the Station are all normal. Nothing to raise any eyebrows, mostly supply data, re-orders and money transfers."

"So you never received any message along the lines of "help we are being attacked!"

The Captain glanced at Edith. That last question was defiantly sarcasm.

She continued. "What about the other space stations your company or your subsidiaries own? I figure you must have at least a dozen."

Hubbard shook his head. "We have no way of knowing. We wouldn't have known about Alpha XP if you hadn't witnessed it. I have had to despatch investigation teams to inspect all of them."

"How long will that take?" Asked The Captain.

"Too long!" Was the answer.

The Captain nodded. "I have an idea!"

Hubbard didn't smile. "Let's see if it matches mine!"

It did!

Chapter Four.

Two days later they were back on board the space station. As not to fall into any temptations, they headed for food and drink of the non alcoholic variety. No one noticed one of their number slip away, just as no one noticed an extra potted palm standing at the edge of the bar area. The rest of the crew lingered over their meals and were the last to leave.

As the lights dimmed the staff tidied up and, once their jobs had been completed, they simply froze where they stood. The potted palm waited. Sure enough after a brief wait, a battle droid appeared at the entrance to the bar. It stopped and scanned the area. Satisfied that everything was as it should be, it passed on. There was no one in the room to notice a potted palm turn into a second battle droid and drift off, following the first.

Once outside the bar the Blue Man followed the battle droid down a series of silent dimmed corridors that led to public spaces. They passed closed cafes, bars, shops and suppliers. Behind each counter The Blue Man could see the android attendants standing motionless in their shut down mode.

Eventually they turned into a second series of corridors. Now they were joined by other battle droids, as if the patrols were all coming together. By the time they entered a large storage hanger The Blue Man was surrounded by at least twenty battle droids. Once inside the hanger there were more of them, lots more, over a hundred. He followed them and stood in line. Nothing moved. After a while he began to wonder if they too had been powered down. Then at the far end of the hanger there was a shimmer and from nowhere a giant screen appeared. It began flashing a series of lines and what looked like numbers. The battle droids began to awake and move. They hovered and shuffled and divided into a number of smaller groups. The Blue Man tagged onto one of the groups and found himself being led down a corridor that led away from the hold. Once again he travelled down a series of corridors until the group passed through a door and into one of the landing stages. In front of him were half a dozen space ships, of all races, all on a stopover, travelling from somewhere to somewhere else. Suddenly the droids began to rise in the sir. The Blue Man watched as they surrounded each of the moored ships. As most of the crews were asleep, or resting, they didn't expect battle droids to force entry into their ships and take prisoners of anyone who didn't put up a fight, which were very few. The crew members who did put up a fight, or show any type of resistance were simply killed where they stood. The Blue Man watched realising with growing horror that the same operation was being carried out in every flight deck on board the space station. He wondered what was happening on board Orcas Teeth.

On the flight deck The Captain watched everything that was happening. The implant in The Blue Man had worked. At first there was some doubt as to whether an encoded implanted comms would continue to work after a shape change had occurred. They had tested it for two days before re-entering the orbit of the space station. At first The Blue Man had objected to a full implanted surveillance of everything he saw and did. It was only when Star assured him it would be turned off during sleep and ablutions breaks. He was grateful for small mercies.

Despite being in an overnight parking place inside the landing stage of a space station, the ship had all screens up full. Down in the weapons pod every safety catch was off and all weapons were fully charged and target locked. As the first battle droids appeared from a passageway Cat Face let them have it. Unable to assess what was happening the droids continued to enter the landing stage only to be blow into smithereens. Soon none of them remained.

The noises from the explosions were loud enough to wake the crews of the other three ships sharing the landing stage. Soon alien faces were seen at the windows of cockpits and at weapons points.

The Captain looked across at Star. "Ready to patch in?"

Star nodded and pressed a switch. The Captain began speaking.

"Fellow Captains, we are under attack. We have dealt with the first attack. However other landing stages have been taken. Many crews have been killed and others taken prisoner. My advice is to prepare yourselves. More battle droids will be on their way."

As he finished speaking he looked across to Star. As if in reply to his unanswered question the landing stage became full of the noise of engines and proto drives being fired up. Two ships burst into life. The first to reach the exterior entrance to the landing platform took off at warp speed. It didn't get far. The explosion lit up the patch of space it once filled. Seeing what had happened, the second ship tried to abort its take off. Unfortunately it couldn't shut down its engines in time. It had barely cleared the landing stage when it exploded in a flash of light and debris. The third ship stayed where it was.

"In coming!" Star said as he punched a button on the comms station.

The image of a lizard like purple man appeared on the screen. It began to speak.

"We have assessed the situation. Escape seems problematical. We propose...."

Whatever he was about to say was cut off as Cat Face shouted and began firing at the entrance to the hold. More battle droids had appeared. The Captain looked up at the screen. The Lizard man had turned away from his comms and was issuing a series of orders. Suddenly the weaponry from his ship burst into life. Between them the two ships accounted for another twenty battle droids.

Back inside the hold of the space station the Blue Man heard the noise of the weapons and watched as more battle droids were despatched in the direction of the battle. Other, smaller groups were despatched towards various corridors. He followed a column of eight down a series of passages until they reached a large circular pillar. The Blue Man realised it was a turbo lift linking the many levels. Without waiting for a lift a battle droid blasted the doors open and entered the shaft. It hovered briefly before sinking down. The other seven followed, heading into the bowels of the station. The Blue Man moved forward and at the last minute moved to one side. Suddenly the droid disappeared. Now the shape shifter chose the form of a large mechanical infantry bot. He turned and rumbled back down the corridor. As he turned a corner he came across another group of battle droids. He didn't hesitate. He lifted the mechanical arm and gripped his hand into a fist. The automatic weaponry fired. All six battle droids were destroyed in one salvo. He carried on down the corridor heading towards the landing stage where Orca's Teeth was moored, hoping against hope that The Captain was still monitoring him.

The Captain wasn't. At that moment he was in a conversation with the Lizard captain. They were discussing what to do next, but as both Captains realised they were trapped, they were not coming up with any constructive ideas. Escape wasn't an option, and it was only a matter of time until the battle droids launched a bigger and heavier attack. They were outnumbered. Star was running a detector program and noticed a group of droids gathering outside the station, at the entrance to the landing pad. Cat Face was in direct contact with his counterpart on the Lizard ship and it had been agreed the Lizard weapons master would cover the passage entrances whilst Cat Face would concentrate on the entrance to the landing stage. He grinned, showing his fangs, as he swung his weapons round. He pressed a couple of buttons and his target finders locked onto the entrance. With fingers on triggers he held his breath and waited for the first sign of movement.

Edith was checking the comms screen linking to the Blue Man and saw his transformation. She checked his movement and realised he was heading towards them. She shouted down into the weapons pod.

"There's an infantry bot on its way. Its Blue Man, tell your Lizard friends not to fire, he's one of us!"

The Blue Man rumbled down a final corridor that opened up into the landing stage. As he entered he saw the Orca at the far end. He began moving towards it when his attention was taken by movement at the entrance to the landing. Very slowly, row after row of battle droids hovered into view and began to make a landing. The first row was met by a bright blue beam coming from the Orca's weapons pod. Then a series of flashes from the proton lasers swept the entrance clear.

A series of explosions from the opposite side of the moorings told him the battle droids were launching a secondary attack from inside the station. He turned and looked back down the corridor he had just travelled. Sure enough he saw a glint of metal. He set himself on his armoured legs and lifted both arms and fired. The end of the corridor exploded in a series of flashes and sparks and then it caught fire. He quickly reversed the bot and rolled across the floor until it reached the Orca. As he waited for the door to open he heard The Captains voice in his ear.

"Actually you're a lot more use out there!"

He cursed himself for not shape shifting quickly enough.

There were two more attacks by the battle droids before they retreated back down the corridors. Star had monitored communications and, with the help of Hubble's people from the SIT, had located full 3D plans of the space station. Now they could see exactly where the battle droids were. Star watched as they divided into small groups that moved around, inside the station. At first he was puzzled. The he realised what he was seeing. He shouted across to The Captain.

"The droids are destroying the place from the

inside!"

The large screen on the flight deck suddenly burst into life. It was Hubble and he wasn't wearing a happy hat.

"Gentlemen I have just received a report. In the last hour six space stations have been attacked. Two are being held to ransom and three have been destroyed. The battle droids destroyed them from the inside and then self destructed."

The Captain said nothing but pressed a couple of buttons. The engines began to throb gently. He turned to Edith.

"Get Blue Man aboard!"

He hit his comms and the image of the Lizard Captain came into view. "You heard?"

The Lizard Captain nodded. The Captain hit another couple of buttons.

"The way I figure it we stand a better chance of getting of this thing if we go together. For one thing they may be too busy wrecking the place to be manning external weapons. Secondly if they are manned we stand a fifty-fifty chance, one of us might get through."

As the Lizard Captain thought the matter through Cat Face cut into the comms.

"Go backwards! That way I can shoot at them as we leave. I'll aim everything I've got up and down, spray everything in sight."

His image closed and from the weapons pod came the sound of switches being clicked.

The Captain looked up at his comms screen. "Backwards it is!"

He checked with Edith. Blue Man was aboard. He gave a countdown. Two engines on two ships roared into life and two ships burst out of the landing stage like corks from a bottle. Their weapons were firing before they left the station, taking out most of the landing stage on their way to the exit. As they shot out into space explosions burst all around them. Both ships were buffeted. The Captain pulled his wheel one way and then another before shooting off on full proton drive at an angle that ensured a maximum distance from the ship being driven by The Lizard Captain.

Inside Orcas Teeth, despite being strapped into their seats, the crew lurched one way and then another. To prevent himself from being thrown around, the Blue Man had shape shifted back into the shape of a potted palm and had jammed himself into a corner where he swayed violently from side to side. Inside his weapons pod Cat Face was strapped in and continued to pour a variety of lasers, and proton beams into the space station.

On his monitor screen The Captain noticed the Lizard Captain had manoeuvred his ship to the other side of the space station. He was still firing.

Suddenly Star shouted out. "Proton drive, full max. Now!"

The Captain didn't hesitate. He pressed a button and the ship was somewhere else. Behind them the blackness of space was illuminated by a huge blinding light. The space station had exploded. Everyone stopped what they were doing to look up at the screen. The Blue Man returned to his normal blue man shape. Edith looked across to the now empty corner.

"I quite liked having a potted palm over there!" She said to no one in particular.

The Captain looked across to Star. His body wobbled as he shrugged. "I picked up an incoming communication to the station. It held a self destruct instruction."

The Captain nodded.

"In coming!" Edith said as she punched a button. The image of Hubble of the SIT faded up on the screen.

"How the hell did you find us? Even I'm not sure where we are, and I'm here!" The Captain remarked acidly.

The Director of Security smiled. There was no humour in it. "Were locked together via your eye patch, remember? I don't have to search for you, I'm with you!"

The Captain gave a little shudder.

The Blue Man turned towards Edith. "Talking of implants."

She nodded and reached for a pair of small tweezers.

"I suggest you leave it where it is!"

They all looked up at the screen. The Director of Security continued. "The implant proved most useful. We gained a lot of information from your transmissions."

The Blue Man looked up at the screen. He wasn't amused. "You mean you continued transmitting whilst I was under cover? Did it never occur to you that you could have been intercepted and my cover compromised?"

The Director of Security looked straight back at him. "We considered it a viable risk!"

The Blue Man swore.

The Captain ignored the interchange. "So what about our commission? We did what was required."

Hubble shook his head. "The mission still stands. We still need to know who commissioned the attack and why. We have two traces to analyse. Once the data has been assessed I will contact you with the information and further instructions."

The screen went blank. Before anyone could say anything Star looked at his screen. "He's still linked via your eye patch." He remarked.

"I hadn't forgotten." The Captain remarked. He looked across the deck towards Edith.

"Damage report." He asked.

She punched a series of buttons and ran some checks.

"Nothing we can't cope with." She answered.

"I need to recharge and re-arm all weapons." Cat Face said from inside the weapons pod.

"We'll stand off for a while." The Captain remarked. He looked across at Star. "Any trace of the Lizard Captain and his ship?"

Star wobbled his head. "I've a feeling he went into hyper drive as soon as he sensed the station was about to explode. Anyway there's no sign of any wreckage."

"How can you tell?" asked The Blue Man.

Star kept looking at his screens and consuls. "I had his co-ordinates fixed. There's nothing there. If he had been hit there would be something there, if only debris."

The Captain looked out at empty space. "Back on our own again!"

"Not with the magic eye of the SIT in your head!" Edith murmured.

"So what happens now?" The Blue Man asked.

The Captain rubbed his chin. "We rest, recharge everything that needs recharging, repair what needs to be repaired and wait until we receive further instructions."

He sighed. "It looks like we have to work hard for our money!"

Chapter Five

It was two days later that the comms kicked into life. As the screen cleared they saw the image of the Director of Security. Standing next to him was a man dressed in an old-style three piece suite. It looked smart and expensive.

"This is Mr Read. He is the chairman of the SIT organisation."

Everyone on the flight deck of The Orca looked at the screen and the man standing there. As long as they had been involved in piracy the man represented the type of person they had made a not too successful career of robbing. To them it was always an added delight to know that somewhere, someone with a lot more money and power was losing, as they were gaining. The man in front of them was the unknown face of the corporation. He was "The Man" they frequently tried to "stick it to". It did cross The Captains mind that suddenly he was now working for "the man", and his corporation. He gave a little shudder. Still ten thousand universal credits were ten thousand universal credits.

He nodded at the Chairman in a sort of acknowledgement. At first the conversation was one sided as the Chairman and his Head of Security began to outline the results of their data search. They had tracked the signals to a small moon orbiting a large gas planet, ten light years towards the edge of the galaxy. As the men spoke Stars screen filled with co-ordinates. He found the moon and locked onto it as the Chairman continued speaking.

"We have despatched fighter ships. They will be there inside three moons. Before they make their approach I would like you to conduct a pre-emptive sweep. Your ship is well shielded, small, and can get in and out quickly. You will liaise with the fleet, they have your co-ordinates so they will be able to track your progress."

"You mean they'll be able to tell if we get blown out of the galaxy and take evasive action?" The Captain said. He wasn't smiling. The Chairman was.

"That would be most unfortunate, especially considering our investment in you. However, I'm sure that anyone who can sneak aboard one of our transporters and help themselves to spare engine parts can sneak up on a small moon!"

The Captain felt like kicking himself. Sometimes he

was too clever for his own good. He looked across at Star.

"Co-ordinates fixed?"

Star shook his head. "We have a slight problem. We can't orbit the moon. The thing is in orbit round that gas planet. Anything trying to orbit the moon will get trapped in the gravity field of the gas planet and sucked down into its atmosphere – then kaboom! Not a nice way to die."

"What's the distance between the two?" The Captain asked.

"Too near!" was the answer.

The Captain thought for a little while. No one spoke. Eventually he looked back at Star. "Find out anything you can about that moon. Find out where the signals are coming from. We need to plot an approach course".

He pressed a lever and the ship moved gently forward.

Throughout the journey Star kept plotting and scanning. He had linked into the SIT comms and scans and co-ordinates passed between the ship and the SIT base. Eventually he punched a button and a close up image appeared on the flight deck screen. Red lines pulsated outwards heading into deep space. A series of yellow lines formed a spiders-web like network around the moon itself. Finally a set of blue lines pulsed and radiated the around the moon.

"The red lines are communications channels. The yellow lines are some sort of protective screening. The blue lines are the direction their scanners are pointing."

He paused to allow the information to sink in. "All in all it's got a very efficient defence and offensive set-up. It'll pick anything up approaching from a light year away at least."

The Captain examined the image. "There's a weak point isn't there?" he said finally.

Star nodded. "There is but it's inaccessible. It's on the moons dark side, right where its closest to the gas planet, where a ship can't get in due to the gravitational pull."

The Captain examined the screen. "I think I can get in there!" he said eventually.

Edith looked at the screen. "To get into position to get around the back of the moon you'll have to find a way past those screens. They fan out of the place like a, a .... well, like a fan actually. It can't be done!"

The Captain smiled. "Not if we make an approach from the far side of the gas planet. If we get as close as we can and go around it. Look!"

He pointed at an area on the edges of the moon. The places where the scanners didn't reach.

"Neither the yellow or blue lines go right around the moon, they don't cover the far side. There's a gap. We aim for that gap, creep under the scans."

"You do realise that the reason there are no screens is that no one in their right mind would even consider flying that close to the gas planet." The Blue Man observed.

"The Captain smiled. "I'm not in my right mind!" He bent down and began pushing buttons He looked up at Star.

"Find me a way in!" he said.

Star nodded.

From a distance the gas planet was a spectacular sight. Great clouds of flaming gasses engulfed the entire sphere. They swirled and flared out into space. The planet itself pulsated and glowed. Looking at the close up images it was terrifying. Great tongues of flame flared out as burning vapours could be seen swirling around in what passed as an atmosphere before bursting into flame. Then there was the invisible danger, the gravitational pull. It took Edith, Star and Cat Face to combine forces and brain power to calculate its strength. The mathematics wasn't made any easier by the fact that the gravitational field wasn't consistent. As the giant flares shot into space they pushed the gravity out in front of them. A paranoid person might think it was reaching out, trying to grab any ship foolish enough to fly near and drag them back into the burning mass of alien gas.

"Any chance of predicting a flare up?" The Captain asked more in hope than in common sense.

Stan an Edith shook their heads. The Blue Man let out a little groan.

"We'll use the old fashioned method then." The Captain said.

"What's that then?" asked The Blue Man.

"We keep our fingers crossed!" The Captain replied and pushed a lever forward.

The ship headed towards the gas planet. Everyone held their breath. As they passed into semi-orbit they could feel the effects of the planet. The forces created by the flares and explosions rocked them. Even inside their ship they could feel the heat.

Cat Face shouted up from the weapons pod. "The paint works getting blistered!"

The Captain ignored him. There wasn't any paint on the outside of the ship. That meant the actual skin of the ship was blistering.

Despite the sweat that was now dripping from his forehead The Captain kept both his hands on the ships wheel. He felt every slight move and made the appropriate adjustments. His one good eye stared at the screen watching as co-ordinates formed a series of lines. The ship turned and lurched with such a force that everyone almost fell over. As they hung onto anything they could they looked at the screen. The gas planet was behind them. In front of them was the bruised and battered surface of the planets moon.

"Stand by to land!" The Captain said through gritted

teeth.

They came in fast and, at the last moment applied the reverse thrusters. The ship almost tore itself apart but it worked, although it made for a very bumpy landing. Star punched buttons and keys as fast as a man with a mechanical hand and sixteen fingers could, which was very fast. He looked up at The Captain.

"We've made it. On the up side, not one beam broken and their shields are all over our heads. On the down side, one of the landing legs is buckled and all our shields are on overheat."

"Let's see what we have to see!" The Captain remarked.

They left the ship in the hands of Edith and Star and climbed down into the hold where they suited up. In the corner was a small hovercraft. They climbed aboard. The air locks kicked into action, the doors opened and the machine flew out, keeping low, barely skimming over the barren rocky surface.

In the ship Star watched his monitors carefully guiding them under the various screens and beams. Eventually he told them to stop. They dismounted and crept to the top of a rocky ridge. Below them were a series of buildings. Lights illuminated a large scale station. They settled down behind a boulder and watched as above them the blue lines of shields sparked and crackled. They seemed to emanate from a small tower at the centre of the station. Cat Face nodded towards it.

"I can take that out!"

The Captain turned to see Cat Face un-strapping a laser guided proton mortar. He held up his hand. "That's only the blue screens. We need to knock out the red and yellow ones as well."

Cat Face peered into the complex. "Can't see their sources!" he said.

"They must be on the other side of the buildings." The Captain remarked.

The Blue Man pointed to where a series of yellow beams met to form a network over the ground buildings. "What would happen if we broke those beams?"

"All hell would break lose!" The Captain said.

The Blue Man nodded and thought for a few

minutes as they all stared at the complex below them.

"Star, how far away are the fighters?"

Instead of Stars voice the vice of Hooper echoed inside all their heads. "If you can eliminate the scanners they can be there inside half a moon."

The Captain didn't need to speak. He just thought the next question. "Too long. We don't even know if they have a fail-safe system."

There was a moments silence then a second voice broke in. It was the Chairman of the SIT. "My people have studied your flight path. Our pilots believe they can follow your course around the gas planet. I have despatched six of the best to follow your route, only they will not land. They are on a bombing and strafing run. As they approach your location knock out the defence shields. It will take co-ordination as they will attack in formation. I strongly advise you to keep your heads down."

The three of them hid behind the boulder and waited, watching the buildings below them. Nothing seemed to be moving, just the coloured beams scanning and crackling above them.

"Fighter ships approaching!" Stars voice echoed inside their heads.

Cat Face lifted his weapon onto his shoulder and took aim. He braced himself against the rock and locked his co-ordinates.

They all became aware of a countdown echoing in their heads. They weren't sure where it was coming from, either Star or the SIT HQ, but they hoped whoever it was knew what they were doing. As it hit zero Cat Face fired his weapon. They watched as the rocket sped towards its target. It was a direct hit, the tower exploded. As sparks, flames and debris shot into the air the network of shields above them began to dissolve. Then suddenly the ground beneath them trembled. They turned just in time to see a fighter ship scream over their heads. They watched as it flew low over the base, spraying the area with ground fire.

Before it disappeared over the horizon it was followed by another five ships flying in formation. The three of them pressed themselves into the ground as the base disappeared in a cloud of smoke and explosions. Burning debris spun and fell around them. The Captain looked up. The sky was clear, there were no more screens or shields to be seen. They picked themselves up just as the fighters circled and came in for another bombing and strafing run. They dropped to the ground once again. As they waited for a third pass a large beam of light burst out from the centre of rubble that was once the complex. Before they could make a comment a ship flashed out, and rode the tractor beam until it disappeared into space.

Cat Face leant back and fired but he was too late. The ship was well out of range and then just wasn't there anymore.

"Someone's in a hurry!" The Captain remarked.

"Do you think there's anyone left alive in there?" The Blue Man asked.

"Call the fighters off and we'll go and find out!" The Captain said.

Once they had heard Stars voice confirming the fighters had withdrawn they stood up and remounted the hovercraft. They flew to a large hole in the outer wall of the building. They stopped, dismounted and drew their weapons, then entered through the hole in the wall. Inside the building small fires were burning. Cables dangled and swung sending showers of sparks dancing along the floor.

Cat Face went first. He stopped and fired his weapon down a corridor. There was an explosion.

"Battle droid!" He said.

The Captain noticed a passageway that seemed to lead deeper inside the building.

"Full scan!" He said into his mouthpiece.

He heard a grunt of acknowledgement from Star. Suddenly he could see a small map inside his head. A little red dot marked his position. The passage seemed to lead into the centre of the complex. He nodded at the others and they set off. As they entered the passage he nodded at The Blue Man who turned into a battle droid. It moved forward and went first.

The passageway was deserted. They followed it around until they reached a large chamber that according to the map marked the centre of the complex. Carefully they looked around. It appeared to have been some type of control centre. Shattered computer screens and banks of smoking controls were scattered across the floor. Cables and wires hung lose, sparking and fizzing. In the centre of the room stood two stationary battle droids, The

Captain pulled his weapons and one of them exploded in pieces. A voice echoed in his head.

"Bring one with you. We may be able to get some information from its data banks."

It was the voice of Hubble, the Director of SIT security. Before he could answer Stars voice broke into his head.

"Initial scans show no sentient life form inside the complex. Clear to go!"

The Captain slid his weapon into its shoulder holster. The Blue Man returned to his human shape. Cat Face had stopped sweeping the area with his weapon and was looking at one of the smoking control panels.

"There's got to be something worth our while around here." He said as he pulled a lose wire. A small transformer fell out of the panel and dropped onto the floor. He looked down at it.

"All sorts of bits and pieces we could use."

The Captain spoke into his headset. "Edith. Grab a hovercraft, a spanner and some wire cutters. Take whatever you think might be useful."

The voice of Hubble echoed in his head once again. "My people will be with you inside an hour. They will take over and carry out any necessary forensic examinations. I'm sure I don't need to remind you but as yet we have no idea who operated or financed this station. They escaped. That was unfortunate!"

Chapter Six

The Captain sat in his seat on the flight deck and
totalled up the profits of his enterprise. Orcas Teeth
now had ten thousand universal credits in its
account. That was good. Edith had spent the last
three days cannibalizing the ships engines and
internal systems, adding and replacing parts she had
salvaged from the space station. Cat Face had found
a new weapons system to play with. The Director of
Security had remained mostly quiet. He was busy
analysing an inspecting the data they had found.
Every so often he had contacted The Captain to ask
opinions and sound out theories. It was during one
of these conversations that he had revealed that the
co-ordination of attacks on the other company space
stations had originated from this complex. He also
revealed that his company had paid a huge amount
of universal credits for the release of the two
remaining space stations. The money had been paid
into an anonymous account and the battle droids on
the stations had just de-powered themselves. They
just turned themselves off and stayed where they
were. The Captain winced, the amount the SIT had
paid would be enough to buy a dozen droid armies.
A meeting had been called. It was on the SIT's
home planet, on the opposite side of the galaxy.
None of them had ever been there before, and none

of them really wanted to go there now, but The Director of Security had promised they would be paid expenses and everyone was eager to test out the new improvements to the ship, so it was a no brainer. That was why some moons later, the crew of Orca's Teeth found themselves being shown into a very plush office on the three hundredth floor of a very prestigious building.

Inside the office were three people, two they already knew, Hubble, The Director of Security and the Chairman of the Organisation, who still appeared not to have a name. Hubble introduced the third person, a short dark haired little man with a nervous twitch. He was the company lawyer. Cat Face let out a small growl. He didn't like lawyers. Edith gave him a sharp nudge in his ribs, just to remind him of his manners.

The Chairman of the SIT looked at the people standing in front of him. A very attractive female android, a large green wobbly man with a mechanical hand, a human cat that didn't like lawyers, and a shape shifter that for reasons beyond his understanding preferred to appear as a blue human male. They were led by a tall human male who wore his hair long, had a beard and an eye patch. He noted that none of them had appeared to dress for the occasion.

"Please sit down. I have a proposition to put to you." The Chairman said.

As they listened to what he had to say their eyes widened. They looked at each other and then at Hubble, then at the lawyer and then back at the Chairman. Then they all looked at The Captain. He wasn't smiling. He was thinking. He had just been offered more universal credits than he could ever have dreamt of earning in his lifetime in the form of a retainer. They were being offered a job. That concept caused him more problems than anyone could have imagined. He had never worked for anyone in his life. He watched as the lawyer pushed a sheet of paper towards him.

"The contract!" he said quietly.

The Captain looked down at it and slowly read the wording. The rest of the crew held their breath. The Captain scan read the top of the document. It looked alright but he was always aware that in life it was the large print that gives and the small print that takes away. As he pushed the paper back across the table he noticed the look of horror on the faces of his shipmates.

"We're pirates, we don't do contracts!" He said.

"What do you do?" Asked the Chairman.

The Captain leaned back in his chair and glanced at his crew, then he turned back to the Chairman.

"We do accords!" he said.

The lawyer picked up the paper, folded it and dropped it into a small metal tube, and smiled.

"An accord will be drawn up to meet your requirements!"

The Captain turned to his crew. They were nodding and smiling.

"We have accord?" He asked.

They continued nodding. Inside he let out a little groan. Now there was no going back.

END.

ABOUT THE AUTHOR

Graham Rhodes has over 40 years experience in writing scripts, plays, books, articles, and creative outlines. He has created concepts and scripts for broadcast television, audio-visual presentations, computer games, film & video productions, web sites, audio-tape, interactive laser-disc, CD-ROM, animations, conferences, multi-media presentations and theatres. He has created specialised scripts for major corporate clients such as Coca Cola, British Aerospace, British Rail, The Co-operative Bank, Bass, Yorkshire Water, York City Council, Provident Finance, Yorkshire Forward, among many others. His knowledge of history helped in the creation of heritage based programs seen in museums and visitor centres throughout the country. They include The Merseyside Museum, The Jorvik Viking Centre, The Scottish Museum of Antiquities, & The Bar Convent Museum of Church History.

He has written scripts for two broadcast television documentaries, a Yorkshire Television religious series and a Beatrix Potter Documentary for Chameleon Films and has written three film scripts, The Rebel Buccaneer, William and Harold 1066, and Rescue (A story of the Whitby Lifeboat) all currently looking for an interested party.

His stage plays have performed in small venues and pubs throughout Yorkshire. "Rambling Boy" was staged at Newcastle's Live Theatre in 2003, starring Newcastle musician Martin Stephenson, whilst "Chasing the Hard-Backed, Black Beetle." won the best drama award at the Northern Stage of the All England Theatre Festival and was performed at the Ilkley Literature Festival. Other work has received staged readings at The West Yorkshire Playhouse, been short listed at the Drama Association of Wales, and at the Liverpool Lesbian and Gay Film Festival.

He also wrote dialogue and story lines for THQ, one of America's biggest games companies, for "X-Beyond the Frontier" and "Yager" both winners of European Game of the Year Awards, and wrote the dialogue for Alan Hanson's Football Game (Codemasters) and many others.

OTHER BOOKS BY GRAHAM RHODES

"Footprints in the Mud of Time, The Alternative Story of York"

"The Collected Poems 1972 – 2016"

"The York Sketch Book." (a book of his drawings)

"The Jazz Detective."

"The View From Inside the Pink Monster."
Autobiography of 1975/78

The Agnes the Witch Series

"A Witch, Her Cat and a Pirate."

"A Witch, Her Cat and the Ship Wreckers."

"A Witch, Her Cat and the Demon Dogs"

"A Witch, Her Cat and a Viking Hoard."

"A Witch Her Cat and The Whistler."

"A Witch, Her Cat and The Vampires."

"A Witch, Her Cat and The Moon People."

Photographic Books

"A Visual History of York." (Book of photographs)

"Leeds Visible History" (A Book of Photographs)

"Harbourside - Scarborough Harbour
(A book of photographs available via Blurb)

"Lost Bicycles."
(A book of photographs of deserted and lost
bicycles available via Blurb)

"Trains of the North Yorkshire Moors."
(A Book of photographs of the engines of the
NYMR available via Blurb)

91350321R00080

Made in the USA
Columbia, SC
20 March 2018